SIREN
Publishing

Ménage Everlasting

HEALING HEARTS
1
Warrior Angel

DIXIE LYNN DWYER

Healing Hearts 1: Warrior Angel

Kai vows to never love another, and now her life's work is to help every soldier in need, every law enforcement officer, every first responder, so that no one is left behind.

Kai is known as the warrior angel, the woman who started Guardians help and has been a life saver to those in need. Helping soldiers get the assistance they need--medical and psychological-- and transitioning back into civilian life, as well as law enforcement officers and others who suffer from PTSD. Kai want to give them hope for a new life, a happy one, yet she has given up on love and accepted to never love again.

The last thing she expects is fall in love with three men that represent everything she fears, and yet everything she is drawn to. After losing her brother, a State Trooper killed in the line of duty, and failing to keep her soldier boyfriend alive as he slowly fell deeper and deeper into depression, she doesn't think she could ever be in a relationship with a soldier or a cop.

Zayn, Thermo, and Selasi have got it all. The emotions, the toughness, Special Forces, law enforcement, PTSD, stubbornness, and then some, but somehow they fall in love.

She's resistant, and it nearly costs her everything.

Genre: Contemporary, Ménage a Trois/Quatre, Romantic Suspense
Length: 39,514 words

HEALING HEARTS 1: WARRIOR ANGEL

Dixie Lynn Dwyer

Siren Publishing, Inc.
www.SirenPublishing.com

A SIREN PUBLISHING BOOK

HEALING HEARTS 1: WARRIOR ANGEL
Copyright © 2018 by Dixie Lynn Dwyer

ISBN: 978-1-64243-303-6

First Publication: May 2018

Cover design by Les Byerley
All art and logo copyright © 2018 by Siren Publishing, Inc.

PUBLISHER
Siren Publishing, Inc.
www.SirenPublishing.com

DEDICATION

Dear readers,

Thank you for purchasing this legal copy of *Warrior Angel*.

I dedicate this series to all the men and women in uniform. Our military, our police, our fire fighters, paramedics and all first responders as well as those that love them and support them.

It isn't easy. Just as they have a calling to protect and serve, those that love them have a calling to be supportive, empathetic and proud. God Bless.

Happy Reading,

HUGS!

Dixie

ABOUT THE AUTHOR

People seem to be more interested in my name than where I get my ideas for my stories from. So I might as well share the story behind my name with all my readers.

My momma was born and raised in New Orleans. At the age of twenty, she met and fell in love with an Irishman named Patrick Riley Dwyer. Needless to say, the family was a bit taken aback by this as they hoped she would marry a family friend. It was a modern day arranged marriage kind of thing and my momma downright refused.

Being that my momma's families were descendants of the original English speaking Southerners, they wanted the family blood line to stay pure. They were wealthy and my father's family was poor.

Despite attempts by my grandpapa to make Patrick leave and destroy the love between them, my parents married. They recently celebrated their sixtieth wedding anniversary.

I am one of six children born to Patrick and Lynn Dwyer. I am a combination of both Irish and a true Southern belle. With a name like Dixie Lynn Dwyer it's no wonder why people are curious about my name.

Just as my parents had a love story of their own, I grew up intrigued by the lifestyles of others. My imagination as well as my need to stray from the straight and narrow made me into the woman I am today.

Enjoy *Warrior Angel* and allow your imagination to soar freely.

For all titles by Dixie Lynn Dwyer, please visit
www.bookstrand.com/dixie-lynn-dwyer

TABLE OF CONTENTS

Healing Hearts 1: Warrior Angel 9

Prologue 9

Chapter One 12

Chapter Two 15

Chapter Three 22

Chapter Four 39

Chapter Five 57

Chapter Six 70

Chapter Seven 86

Chapter Eight 97

Chapter Nine 111

Chapter Ten 117

Chapter Eleven 128

Healing Hearts 1: Warrior Angel

DIXIE LYNN DWYER
Copyright © 2018

Prologue

"I love you so much, Edison. We'll get through this. Together, I know we'll get through this," Kai Devaro whispered. She pressed her lips against his head as he rocked slightly against her. He was shaking. She could feel it, and a tear escaped her eye. She was trying so hard not to cry. To not let him know that this was killing her, to see such a strong, amazing soldier, boyfriend, and future husband feeling such pain. That twinge of fear caused an unsettling in her gut. She tried not to show that either. Afraid of the violent side to these things, and what his hands could do to her when he was out of his mind. She squeezed her eyes tight and breathed softly, remaining calm as she learned to do.

Edison tilted his face up toward her. She was holding him from behind on the rug, right next to the bed. She pressed her lips to his forehead. He closed his eyes. Held him in her arms as he stared at the wall, having another one of those episodes. An episode? Why did the doctors call them that? How did zoning out, getting lost in thought, turn into episodes? Being violent one minute and the next crying and rolled up into a fetal position. She caressed him, held him close, and he was so much bigger than her. His muscles huge. His body more than a foot and a few inches taller than hers—a masculine soldier, a trained killer—and he lay in her arms like a small child. It upset her, but it killed him inside for her to see him like this. She just knew it.

He begged her to leave him. To be free of his abuse, of the emotional and physical damage he had done to her over the year, and yet she remained. She knew it wasn't his fault. He didn't mean to strike at her, especially in bed at night when the demons attacked his mind.

She smoothed her hands along his arm and lay her palm against his chest. His heart raced. He was getting weaker and weaker inside, but on the outside, he still appeared a warrior.

She prayed for her lover's return. For him to be whole again. Masculine again. Unafraid of anything or anyone, and a force to be reckoned with. He was sexy, intimidating, powerful and capable. She longed for the love, the desire, the compassion and the care once again. She wanted and needed her lover back. The man she gave her heart and soul to. The only lover she had or would ever have. Why was this happening? Why, when he had been done with the military. Had survived his tours of duty and finally gave it up after nearly dying out there in the Middle East? She thought of the scar along his leg. The battle wounds and the fact that he survived when others hadn't.

God brought him back to her, but he wasn't the same man. He wasn't whole. Where was her Edison? Where was the man who could hold her in his arms and make her feel safe, protected, and beautiful?

His words cut through her heart *"Move on, Kai. You need a real man. I'm all fucked up. You deserve better."*

"I love you," she whispered.

He didn't respond at first, and that hurt. He would always respond, and quickly, and with a hug, a kiss, a caress along her curves, but not anymore. He was giving up, and she was his lifeline.

"Why?" he replied.

"You know why, soldier. We've been together since high school. You're my best friend. My everything. I'm not going anywhere." She caressed his arm and hugged him against her front.

"Why can't he just let me die? I want to die, Kai. I can't take it anymore. I can't," he mumbled, and the tears fell from her eyes.

He was getting worse, and there was no one to help her or to help him with his Post-traumatic stress disorder. He risked his life for this country, he sacrificed everything, and the doctors did nothing. Edison was heading toward a psych ward, or to his grave. He had been there for her. Held her, comforted her when her brother, Peter, was killed in the line of duty serving as a state trooper. What was she going to do? What more could she do for Edison, the man she loved? The man she stood by through every tour and every injury and near death experience? What? The tears flowed and her heart ached.

She never felt so helpless and alone in her life, even as she held her lover, her best friend in her arms. She was alone, and life didn't seem worth living.

Chapter One

"It's quiet," Selasi Stelling whispered to his brother Zayn. They were hiding in the brush under the trees about a hundred yards from the facility they were about to infiltrate. Their other brother, Thermo, along with a few soldiers from another troop, were being held prisoner inside the building. A secret mission gone badly, and the government wasn't sending anyone in to rescue them. So Selasi and Zayn called up their friends, used their connections, and decided to do their own secret mission. They weren't letting their brother die.

The building, a two-story shit hole that looked like it could collapse at the next big windstorm, was heavily guarded. Thermo had been assigned to a special operations unit six months prior. It was supposed to be the last assignment for their brother and then he was retiring from the Corp. Same for Zayn and Selasi, who already got things started with careers after the military. Zayn with the state police as a special training officer and investigator, and Selasi assisting with intel and operations for their buddies who were mercenaries. Zayn and Selasi were done eight weeks ago, and then they got word that Thermo had been captured by a small terrorist cell in Baghdad. It took a lot of finagling and favors to get the info they needed, never mind resourcefulness and a bit of muscle to find the location. They did it though, and without government support, without funding or assistance, except from friends of theirs who were mercenaries.

Selasi swallowed hard, and Zayn exhaled.

"No matter what, don't get dead, bro. We get Thermo out and we never have to come to a shit fucking country like this ever again."

"Agreed." Selasi heard the signal.

"Game time," Zayn whispered, and they got up, pulled their weapons to their shoulders, and slowly crossed the darkness of the open area before the building. Mike, Turner, Fogerty, Watson, Dell, and Phantom were on the move and infiltrating the area. A moment later, gunfire erupted, and Zayn and Selasi hurried to the door where they believed their brother was being held. As men came running out firing their weapons, they returned fire.

"We're coming for you, bro. Just hold tight, Selasi and I are here. We're gonna take you home."

Pop, pop, pop.

* * * *

Thermo barely registered the sound of rapid gunfire. He was left to bleed out, like the others before him, his fellow soldiers and prisoners to these monsters. He heard the guards yelling in their language, and it was obvious the fire wasn't friendly. Could someone be coming in to rescue them? Well him. He was the last one left. All six-feet-five of muscles, steel, had held up against the brutal abuse and starvation. He closed his eyes, his face against the dirt floor as blood dripped from his nose and lips. His chest burned with scars from the blades of knives and the sharp snap of long sticks like whips against his flesh. His nostrils no longer burned from inhaling dirt and the stench of death. His eyes were heavy, not glossy, because he was beyond dehydrated. He was dying, his kidneys failing, and could smell death coming.

His head felt fuzzy, and it was beyond the results of getting knocked around with the butt of guns, slapped, punched and even kicked by heavy, black military boots. His will to live and to fight on was hanging by a thread. As he listened, trying to determine if it was real or a hallucination, the shots came through the door and took one of the guards out.

He watched, still not able to lift his head, still feeling like he was dreaming and this wasn't real, or willing to put what last bit of energy he had into a hallucination of his mind.

More yelling. Thermo felt about an ounce of hope and attempted to move. He slid his palm along the ground to gain leverage, then lifted his aching cheek up off the floor, but he was so damn weak his head fell back to the hard, dirty surface. His nostrils flared. More gunfire, an explosion, and one of the guys fell back into the area where Thermo lay. He was bleeding from his neck and chest, the gun he held lay right there inches from Thermo. That hope he had grew.

He stared at the weapon. The weeks or months that passed never gave him the opportunity to come this close to a weapon, a means to fight and escape. Now it was here and he was so fucking weak from injuries and abuse, he couldn't fucking move.

"Mother fucker. I'm not dying without taking some of these scumbags with me. I'm not." He grunted. He thought of the others. The men who came on the mission with him and who died here. He growled and fought against the pain, the exhaustion, and reached for the AK 47. *I'm a fucking Marine. Special fucking Forces. Death before dishonor. Semper Fi.*

More yelling, then men flooded back into the room. They were shooting through the open windows and the doorway, and he knew this was it. Kill them and die knowing he took the enemy out. Nothing else mattered but seeking revenge so that the other U.S. soldiers' deaths had meaning, and to make those friends proud. Bullets snapped around him, hitting the dirt, ricocheting against the walls inside the room. Whoever was returning fire might wind up killing him by a stray fucking bullet. He had to take these men out.

Thermo shook terribly, and barely had the strength to hold the weapon the right way and place his fingers on the trigger. He cursed and dug deep. The sound of the "pops" echoed in the building and the enemy soldiers dropped one by one. When they were all dead, weakness overtook the will to do more and to just live. His face fell against the gun and the floor. He was breathing slowly.

"Thermo! Thermo?" He blinked his eyes open and he thought he was dreaming. *Selasi and Zayn? My brothers?*

I'm dead. I must be dead.

Chapter Two

Two years later, South Carolina

"Hello?"

"Wow, I actually got you on the phone. Holy shit. Is everything okay?" Afina Stelling asked her friend, Kai.

"Ha, ha, ha. Very funny, Afina. What is going on?"

"You tell me? It's been over a year since you moved out here, and we haven't gotten together to hang out much at all. I thought the whole point of leaving New Jersey was for us to be closer."

"I know, I know. We did coffee several times and even dinner," Kai replied.

"Which you sneakily took off as soon as some of my other friends came around."

"I didn't sneak off. The job is demanding. I'm up to my neck in contracts and negotiations, and having to go to these damn dinner parties to smooze the board members to get money for the facility."

"Oh how dreadful, to have to wear ball gowns, eat caviar, and dance among the wealthy and famous. If I didn't know you so well, I would think their snobbiness had rubbed off on you and you don't want to be seen with us simple folk."

"Cut it out."

Afina chuckled. "I'm just busting your chops. I know you're a workaholic. So, you're finalizing the deal this week, how about meeting me at Corporal's tomorrow night? It's going to be a fun night. All the girls are going, plus, not that you care, but a lot of hot guys hang out there."

"Afina, I think I'll pass."

"No, no, no, you have to come. My brother Mike is going to be there and he hasn't seen you at all."

"Mike? I thought him and his buddies were on another secret job or something."

"They were and just returned. Turner was a little messed up."

"Bad?" Kai asked, instantly feeling nervous and sick to her stomach.

"No, just a black eye and bruised cheek. Mike said it was no big deal."

"I bet. I don't know if I want to go."

"Oh come on, you always have fun with us, besides, Amelia needs us."

"What's wrong? I only saw her for a few minutes yesterday at work in the office at the hospital."

"Cavanaugh, what else."

"Oh no, please don't tell me that she wants to get back together with him."

"I think she is considering it. He's breaking her down. Calls all the time, sends things to her apartment."

"I need to talk to her."

"We do, so bring her to Corporal's tomorrow night. Hey, that surgeon still hitting you up?"

"Nice, Afina. What do you think?"

"That you are out of your mind to not say yes to a date, hell, to sex. It's been three years, Kai."

"Afina."

"I know, I know, you don't date, don't feel capable of being intimate or getting involved with another man, and I get the pain you went through and the loss. I do, but you're young, gorgeous, intelligent and sweet, plus can totally take care of yourself, which means no dickhead like Cavanaugh could manipulate his way into your life. I say use the sexy, hot surgeon for sex."

"Oh brother, here we go. I swear I think you have the hots for him."

"Girlfriend, any sane woman would have the hots for Dr. Chadwick Hayes. He's the number one emergency surgeon in the country, never mind here in South Carolina. He was in the U.S. military academy, so he has that whole discipline, macho sex appeal we're all attracted to, and he's rich."

"He knows all of that, too. No thank you. We're just friends."

"Could make it friends with benefits."

"You are relentless, you know that?"

"Yup. Just trying to hook my girlfriend up with the perfect guy."

"I'm not attracted to him like that."

"You would make an awesome couple. He's all big-time medical doctor raking in the big bucks and you're the good doer, organizing and building up for a nonprofit organization that helps injured and recovering soldiers, and now even first responders. Two philanthropists with enough money to change the world. How awesome would that be? Plus, he could throw some money your way."

"Do you sit at your desk during the day and dream up these crazy fantasies of yours? Him and I are not going to happen. He has been a great contributor already."

"Because he wants you in his bed, and so do his brothers."

"Oh for crying out loud. Seriously, Afina?"

"You know that is how things work around here. Besides, they are just as attractive and major catches, too. You could handle the four of them."

"I can't handle more than one man. Hell, I can't handle even thinking about going out on a date, or getting close to a man. I'm not ready."

Afina sighed. "You're more than ready. It's just going to take meeting the right men to get you ready."

"Not men."

"So tomorrow night?"

"Yes, I'll be there."

"Good, and make sure you tell Amelia and bring her, too. We need to get that girl's mind off that asshole Cavanaugh."

"Will do. Talk to you later."

* * * *

Kai ended the call and then leaned back in her office chair. It was a decent sized office tucked in the corner of the Human Resources Department wing of the hospital, but still an office. A long way from her hole in the wall apartment with spreadsheets, bills, disorganized mess of papers, legal documents, and other things at her fingertips to push for services for injured soldiers, or ones suffering from PTSD and other psychological effects. Now, three years later, and she had set up additional offices with people assisting law enforcement officers, firefighters, and other first responders who needed assistance after injury or other problems. She learned how to negotiate to get donations, and also funding for advertising, and even the newest project, a facility thirty minutes out of town that would be a retreat for recovering soldiers with a full staff of medical personnel to help those individuals get through their PTSD and other psychological problems. All in a relaxed, supportive setting. She felt tears in her eyes. Her goals and dreams of helping to provide a safe haven, a valued resource to save lives instead of losing them to suicide was becoming a reality. One soldier, one police officer, one first responder at a time.

She looked at her desk and the multiple new files that had landed there. Cases that were lost in the shuffle, or minimized because of ancient protocols from nearby hospitals. Kai had gained a reputation as a supporter, an advocate for soldiers and first responders. She was branching out to other organizations and putting together new ideas, and new services that could help the clients. Warrior Angel was the nickname that slowly began to circulate through the network of supporters. She chuckled at the thought. She had gone through so much, had sacrificed everything, and was nearly out of money when she got that first big donation. Canton Shaden, a business tycoon, who lost a son who was in the military and committed suicide, and had three other sons involved in both the military and law enforcement. He flew her out to meet him in person, and he and his wife became great friends, well more like family. Their one son, Keono, had been in a dark place when he returned from serving, and his father found out about Kai's special program and contacted her. Keono had become a good friend to her. In fact, she should give him a call to see how he was doing in the new job.

Kai's door was open and she could hear the women outside talking at their desks discussing their plans for the weekend. She didn't make plans. When she wasn't working, she thought about work and planned out ideas to improve things, or to expand. She went for runs four times a week, and had thought about checking out one of the local dojos in town that offered a bunch of classes, but she didn't want to socialize. She didn't want people to ask her questions. To learn of her life, and of her being single. It took the last year to convince Amelia's aunt Fay that Kai didn't need to be set up on a blind date and that she chose not to date. Kai was asked out often. She declined every time. She wasn't ready. She might never be ready. That heavy sensation fell over her heart. Then came the emptiness that was still there. She thought of him. Of Edison's smile, and not the scene she walked in on. Every soldier she met she thought of Edison, and what could have been if only there were resources available to help, and the right words to say, the right treatment to have access to. That was what hurt and kept her from moving on. She realized that not every person could be saved, but she didn't accept it. She wanted to change that. She would dedicate her life to changing the statistics. More soldiers would live and not die from PTSD.

Tears stung her eyes, three years later and almost as deeply, definitely still traumatized by the crime scene, the police investigation, the sorrowful expressions, and the mourning process of losing the only man she ever loved, and was forever asking why?

She stood up, pushed aside her emotions, the sadness, the loneliness, the fears she lived with mostly at night when she was alone, and she refocused on the next task, the next responsibility, and how she needed to talk to Amelia about tomorrow night.

"Hi, Kai, are you heading out early to get ready for the meeting?" Mel asked.

"I wasn't planning on it, but I think I will. I need you to do me a favor and schedule this case for Lawrence and Olivia. I think they can definitely help this client out," she said, and handed over the file to Mel.

"I will take care of it. Enjoy tonight, and the weekend," Mel said, and winked then walked back to her desk.

That was one thing that Kai had become good at. Hiding her emotions, putting up a fake smile and getting through life alone. By Monday everyone would be talking about their weekend and what fun things they did, and Kai would avoid it all. She made sure to schedule out of the office appointments Monday, and so far it worked.

She looked around, then grabbed her bag and her cell phone. All her work was done. In fact, she was so far ahead of her responsibilities that she didn't have to come to work tomorrow. What would she do though? She could get together with Afina before Corporal's. She could go for a longer run, or maybe check out the classes at that dojo? She had the schedule. Casey's boyfriend worked the front desk there and could get her in for free try. She glanced out toward the main office, and saw Casey smiling and talking on her cell phone while also typing on the computer. That woman could multitask and then some. She debated about asking her and then thought better of it.

Her plan to leave New Jersey and take on this role here closer to her best friend Afina had been a difficult one, but a necessary one. She was drowning in her own sorrows and loss. First of her brother, gunned down by some anti cop mental case, and then the loss of Edison. She gulped. If there had been help, better services available, he wouldn't have become a statistic.

"Hey, you getting ready for the banquet?" Amelia asked her, coming from the hallway.

"Yes. I have to leave in a few minutes. Listen, I just got off the phone with Afina. She wants us to meet her at Corporal's tomorrow night to celebrate and to hang out. You up for it?"

"Uhm." Amelia looked around her and then exhaled. She didn't like hanging out much either. Especially after breaking up with her boyfriend, Cavanaugh. Amelia made a few comments here and there about him being a jerk, very controlling and abusive, that was why she broke things off, but Kai hadn't asked her any questions. She didn't want to push for information and so Amelia didn't push Kai for information from her. She was fine with that.

"We can go together and we don't have to stay long," Kai said to her.

"I can meet you there, you know in case you're having a good time and I'm not and want to leave."

"The likelihood is slim. I haven't gone out much since moving here."

"Well, you've been working here and this new position and expanding the services. It's a good idea to celebrate your hard work."

"Our hard work, Amelia. You've been by my side almost since day one."

"Don't remind me about Beth. She was such an idiot, and so pissed she got fired."

"Well she wasn't doing what she was supposed to and clients suffered. That's unacceptable. We're all they have as advocates."

"Yes we are. So what time tomorrow night?"

"I guess like eight."

"Okay. I'll meet you in the parking lot."

Chapter Three

"What's that look for?" Zayn asked Selasi as he walked into the kitchen and set his duffle bag down on the chair.

"I thought you were getting in last night," Selasi asked.

"Got caught up in a case with Turner's cousins. Had to issue these warrants when a call came on about that guy Banks they were looking for since last May."

"Was it crazy?" Selasi asked.

"Eh. Could have been a situation."

"Everyone okay?" Thermo asked, walking into the kitchen and looking pissed off as usual. He didn't think his brother even knew how to smile.

"Everyone is fine. I know the team has had some close calls lately, but as long as everyone does their jobs then no problems," Zayn said to them.

"Easier said than done. Was Devin involved, too?" Selasi asked about their cousin. He worked undercover in narcotics and warrants, too.

"He was there with his team as backup just in case. He said Mike got back two days ago. They're all looking to hang out at Corporal's tonight," Zayn told them.

Devin was their cousin, as well as Mike and Afina.

"Like a fucking family reunion?" Selasi replied, and Zayn chuckled.

"Don't be surprised when you get a call from Afina. There's some sort of special fundraising event going on there tonight, too. It will be good to hang out."

"We've declined since coming here. Why go tonight?" Thermo said.

"Our cousins will be there, Mike and a few of the guys that we all know. The organization is the one that helped Felix and his family. It's a good cause. It will be fun," Zayn said.

"It will be fucking boring. Same shit. Same war stories from the local cops," Thermo stated.

"You just don't like getting hit on," Selasi teased, and Zayn laughed but Thermo flipped Selasi the middle finger.

"I guess you're still aggravated at that Gloria chick?" Selasi asked.

"Whose great idea was it to send her over to talk to me?" Thermo asked.

"I can assure you that at this point, every fucking woman who lives in this town knows to stay far away from you. You made it clear you aren't interested in getting involved with anyone," Selasi said to him.

"Well he's cramping our style. I think there are some pretty good looking women around town," Zayn said.

"Stalking women. Women out to land a fantasy," Thermo said.

"Who gives a shit if they're open to fooling around no strings attached?" Selasi asked.

"The three of us care. That's the fucking problem. It doesn't matter anyway. We're going to hang out with our cousins and their friends, enjoy a Friday night and relax. No work all weekend for me, so I'm good to go."

"I have some training sessions at the gym for a couple of the guys from the department. Friends of Devin's actually," Zayn said.

"You still need my help?" Thermo asked.

"If you're up to it. I thought you had plans Sunday," Selasi said.

"I do, but in the afternoon. I'll do it. I don't have anything going on right now with Mike and the crew coming back from their last job."

"Good. Then we'll go together.

"Awesome, and tonight, let's try to have fun," Zayn said.

Selasi leaned back in his chair and smiled. "I'm always ready to have fun."

* * * *

Kai walked into Corporal's along with Amelia, who she met out in the parking lot. The place was crowded already and the live band could be heard from outside. It was a warm night, and a lot of the patrons were by the side tiki bar and outdoor deck. Corporal's was a cool place. Not only because of the atmosphere, but also of the types of people who hung out here. The owners, Ghost and Cosmo, were jarheads. The patriotic theme throughout the place was welcoming with old memorabilia from across the United States and even out of the country. A lot of soldiers retired from service and then got into law enforcement or investigative work, so the memorabilia tied it all in.

Kai felt the eyes on her and Amelia the moment they walked through the front door. She had been told over the years how beautiful she was, and especially by Edison, but he was biased. Nowadays it kind of made her feel uncomfortable because she was trying to just slide through life, through the social aspect of it anyway, and just live and take it a day at a time. More recently, with a push from Amelia and Afina, plus Afina's other girlfriends, she wondered if she would ever be able to let a guy close enough. As soon as she thought that, she felt the anxiety and cleared her head.

"Oh boy, you are getting some major looks right now, Kai. I don't know why you don't want to date anyone."

"I think they're looking at you."

"No, not me. It's you. You just don't see it."

"Look, there's Afina," Kai said, avoiding another conversation where her friend or friends informed her about how gorgeous she was and how she was wasting her youth away by remaining single.

"I didn't know that April and North would be here, too," Amelia said to her.

"Looks like everyone is, and Mike, too," Kai said, and they headed toward them. She was excited to see Mike. She hadn't seen him in over a year, but as he turned around, her eyes locked onto the man he was talking to. She nearly paused. His eyes looked right at her, then over her body, and what was that? She felt something. She was shocked and annoyed, but then Mike was calling out her name and lifting her up in the air, twirling her around as she hugged him tight.

"Mike." She laughed and held onto him as he lowered her feet to the floor, but kept his strong, muscular arm around her waist and pulled her toward the bar and the guys there.

"Everyone, meet Kai Devaro," he said and squeezed her against him. The guy she locked gazes with slid off the bar stool to stand up, and holy God was he tall. She tilted her head back and he reached out his hand while stepping closer.

"Zayn Stelling," he said, and she shook his hand as Mike released her. She heard Mike chuckle.

"Stelling? Wait, you're related to Mike and Afina?" she asked.

"Cousin," Mike said, and Kai pulled back and looked behind her to see Amelia standing there with Afina, and both were smirking. Had they noticed her reaction to the good-looking guy? Great, now they would be pushing her to talk to him. That nervous, uncomfortable feeling started to simmer.

"This is Amelia." Kai introduced her and she stepped back, and Amelia shook Zayn's hand hello. Zayn was very attractive. Like model in a military calendar attractive with his crew cut hair, the front spiked up and a very trimmed, short beard, and big dark eyes. Like Liam Hemsworth, but older, more seasoned. He was muscular and at least six-feet-four if she had to guess. He was complete intimidation and she couldn't believe how her body felt. She was annoyed with herself as guilt hit her insides, until Afina was pulling her closer to the bar and near him and Mike plus a few other guys gathered closer.

She was listening to them talk about some case their other cousin Devin had and that apparently Zayn helped out with.

"So you are in law enforcement, too?" she asked, and then took a sip from the glass of rum and soda Mike had gotten for her.

"Sort of. I'm a trainer for investigative procedures and handling the physical aspect of issuing search warrants in arrests."

"He's bad ass, Kai. Don't let him fool you and act all modest. His techniques save lives," Mike said, and Zayn looked away, his expression seemingly embarrassed at the compliment.

"Well, that's a good thing then. The job is dangerous so any good training that can help protect those serving in the department is a positive, right," she said, and Mike agreed.

Zayn looked back at her. "What about you? What do you do?"

"The Warrior Angel, what doesn't she do?" Mike said, and winked at her as he gave her shoulder a squeeze. He was partially standing behind her seat and next to the bar.

"Mike," she reprimanded.

"Modest, too. She runs Guardians Hope. Well, actually, she created it, got the funding for it, and is now chief operating officer for it, isn't that your title, Kai?" Mike asked.

"Wait, that's the organization that helps soldiers and first responders, right? Every department talks so highly of that charity," Zayn said.

"Well, Kai started it all. In fact, I do believe that the fundraising we have going on here tonight is donating part of the money raised to help with one of the shelter programs you started."

She turned to look at Mike. "Seriously? Where did you hear that?"

"Ghost told me. Wait until he sees that you're here."

She looked around for him. "It's been months since I saw him. Where is he I wonder?"

A few other guys came over to talk to Mike and she got up off her seat when one of them was slapping another guy hello on his back and he bumped into her. She felt the hands go to her hips and she gasped, and placed her hands on Zayn's chest and stared up at him.

"Here, have a seat, and I'll stand so no one can bump into you again," he said, and stood up.

Holy God she needed to get away from him. She was not expecting a reaction, an attraction to a man, and here she was staring at Zayn.

"Who do we have here?" She heard another male voice, then felt a hand on her hip. She turned and had to look up like she did with Zayn. Her eyes landed on another really tall man, almost exact height as Zayn, and the deepest blue eyes she had ever seen. He widened his eyes, and then squinted at her as if he felt something by looking and also touching her. She gulped, realizing his hand was huge against her hip, and warm, too. He had dirty blond hair, was clean-shaven, and those dark eyes roamed over her body. The crowd of guys next to them grew bigger, louder with laughter, making it too hard for her to hear what Zayn just said to her, and the second guy pressed closer and she was now sandwiched between them. Holy God she felt overheated, aroused and no way protected.

"Damn it's crowded."

"Kai, meet my brother, Selasi," Zayn said, and she almost blurted out an 'oh shit', but instead she smiled, pressed Selasi's hand off her hip, and then put some space between the two men and her.

She was leaning against the bar. "Nice to meet you," she said, and Selasi reached his hand out for her to take. When their fingers touched, she felt the same powerful attraction. She pulled her hand back and looked around for Afina, Amelia, someone.

More laughter erupted and Mike was coming back over.

"Damn I forget how fun this place is. Hey, is Thermo here?" Mike asked, and she didn't know who he was talking about, but she was grateful for the distraction from the two men. Mike squinted as Selasi spoke, his eyes glancing back at her with interest.

"He found his spot by the corner of the bar. You know how he hates crowds," Selasi said, and then Zayn handed him a bottle of Bud Lite.

"Thanks, bro. So, Kai, that's a nice name. You live around here?" he asked, and Mike chuckled.

"What?"

"Maybe I should go keep Amelia company. I kind of dragged her here tonight," Kai said, and then stepped forward to look past the crowd of men. She felt the hand on her waist. "Don't go. Talk to us. If you leave, then we'll be stuck hearing one of Mike's war stories," Zayn said, and winked.

"Nice. What about your war stories? Listen, Kai won't be impressed or shocked by any stories. She's heard a lot of them," Mike said.

She could feel Selasi and Zayn's eyes on her, and of course something tingling inside. An awareness, and well an attraction. It was unnerving, and she truly didn't know how to handle this. She avoided when men flirted and especially soldiers. As much as Afina, Amelia, and her friends pushed for her to get into the dating scene, Kai just couldn't. She had no interest, so why was she glancing at Zayn and Selasi every chance she got?

"Why is that?" Zayn asked.

"She's been around soldiers and cops all her life. You won't impress her. In fact, I've been trying to impress her for years and finally gave up," Mike teased, giving her a wink. She chuckled.

"How do you know Kai?" Selasi asked Mike.

Mike looked at her and smiled. "Kai and Afina have been friends for years. They were in college together in New Jersey, at Seton Hall. I went to visit a few times."

"You came to check up on Afina?" Kai asked, and smiled.

Mike stepped closer to her and put his hands on her hips and pulled her close. "I went to hit on my little sister's best friend."

"You're such an idiot," Kai said, laughing and shoving him back.

He chuckled and stepped back but looked her over. "You know I tried."

"I didn't deny you did."

"Wait, you two were a thing?" Zayn asked, and he looked a little serious.

"No. Never even got the opportunity to kiss the woman."

She hoped he didn't bring up Edison. "Well, you got yourself in enough trouble by hitting on Miss Bradshaw. If I recall correctly, you were banned from the campus for starting a fight," she said, and Mike shook his head, turned red and then looked away.

"Who is Miss Bradshaw?" Selasi asked.

"Afina's accounting teacher at the time, who Mike here decided to pick up in a bar down the block from the campus, and well, he got her drunk, brought her to campus and a rowdy party he instigated and that's where the fight broke out.

"Oh shit. Seriously? Did Afina get in trouble or get a bad grade?" Zayn asked.

"Are you fucking kidding me? My sister was getting straight A's and that would continue. I'm that good. See what you missed out on, sexy," Mike teased her, giving her hip a tap.

"You are so full of crap," Kai said, and Mike started laughing.

"Hey, it was fun."

"It was fun. Good times," Kai said, but then looked away, her mind back onto all the bad memories that overshadowed the good ones.

Kai listened as Selasi, Mike, and Zayn talked about the local dojo and some additional classes being offered, and she took the opportunity to watch the men and realized she needed to mingle with her friends. It was safer than making these guys think she wanted them to flirt with her or she was interested. Getting involved with a man was the last thing on her mind, but then Mike brought up the private sessions.

"Wait, they offer those at the dojo?" she asked.

"Well, they're more for experienced martial artists. A lot of the law enforcement guys do them to stay sharp," Mike said to her.

"Oh, I was going to check out the classes there this week to see what they offered because I heard there was Muay Thai, but beginners," she said to them.

"You do Muay Thai?" Zayn asked her.

"She's been doing that for years. I thought Afina said you gave that up a year ago," Mike said.

"I got busy with the new job and working so many hours. I want to get back into it, but I'm not interested in beginners' classes."

"Selasi does a private session with three guys from Devin's division with the state police," Mike said to her.

"How is Devin?"

"He's here tonight. You haven't seen him?"

"No." She looked around them.

"Last I saw him he had a few women fussing over his bruises," Zayn said, and took another slug from his bottle of Bud Lite.

"Bruises?" Kai asked with concern.

"He's okay. Just got into a little scuffle with some guys who were trying to stop him from serving a warrant," Mike told her.

She wasn't surprised but she did feel a bit upset. She feared for these guys. For the men and women in the service of law enforcement and the danger they were in on a regular basis. Another reason why she would never and could never see herself involved with a cop or a soldier ever again.

"Kai!" She heard her name and looked past the guys and saw Ghost standing there. He was six feet tall, older Marine with gray crewcut hair and muscles galore. He worked out and trained all the time, and boy did he have a personality on him.

"Excuse me please," she said, and walked toward Ghost who pulled her into his arms and then started walking her away. She glanced over her shoulder and saw Zayn and Selasi watching her. She quickly looked back. She really needed to stay clear of them. The whole attraction thing surprised her.

"I heard you got a nice donation last night to the soldiers' retreat," he said to her.

"How did you hear about that?"

"Sweetie, I have backed your ideas since the first night we met here more than a year ago. What you have accomplished is simply amazing."

"Not on my own though, Ghost. With supporters like you, your buddies and families who truly need the help, and Canton, of course."

"So, how do you know Zayn and Selasi?" he asked.

"I just met them."

"Oh, they're good men. Retired soldiers, Special Forces actually." Her heart pounded inside of her chest. "They don't come here too often," he said and stared at her.

"What?"

He squinted.

"What?" she repeated, but then he placed his hand on her shoulder and turned her toward the other end of the bar.

"There's someone I would like you to meet."

* * * *

"Gorgeous, isn't she?" Mike said to Zayn and Selasi.

Zayn was watching Kai walk farther away from them and toward the other end of the bar. He glanced at Selasi. "Who?"

"You know damn straight who. Kai. Isn't she fucking hot? I'm a pretty good-looking guy, and I don't have any problems getting women, but holy shit, even I'm intimidated around her."

"Intimidated?" Selasi asked.

"You know what I mean," Mike said, and then stepped closer and looked around them. "The woman has guys asking her out all the time. She says no. I've known her for years, and yeah, been away more often than not, but she doesn't accept any dates."

"Why is that?" Zayn asked.

"Well, she dated a guy through high school and college. He was a Marine."

Zayn squinted. "He broke her heart or something?"

"Came back all fucked up. I never got all the details, but he died. Killed himself and she was never the same. Moved out here a couple of years ago, and I swear the woman is on a mission to save every soldier or cop with PTSD." He took a slug of beer.

"Damn, I hate hearing about that shit. Especially when things were bad for Thermo for a while," Selasi said to them.

"How is he doing? Seems a lot better as far as when myself or the guys ask for his help on a mission, but I mean he isn't right here with the guys. He's in a corner."

"He's here though, and not at home alone. He just doesn't like socializing," Zayn said.

"Women throw themselves at him with all those tats and that beard and dark look in his eyes. The man could be working that shit," Mike said and chuckled.

"No. It would take something major for him to even take notice," Selasi said.

"Well, I know the team and I are glad you guys moved back here after retiring, and Devin is definitely happy, Zayn." Mike chuckled.

"He tells me all the time. His job is pretty damn dangerous."

"It takes a special kind of cop, but Devin is a natural."

* * * *

"I would like you to meet my good friend Clover. He's been helping to organize the fundraiser this evening and doing a great job, I might add," Ghost said.

Kai smiled and reached her hand out for him to shake. He was an attractive older man with gray hair and was tall and bulky like Ghost.

"The Warrior Angel? In the flesh?" Clover asked.

She chuckled and then glanced at Ghost. "Who exactly started that whole Warrior Angel thing anyway?" She winked.

"Obviously you are well loved and appreciated," Ghost told her.

She noticed some really big, scary looking guy sitting on a stool at the corner of the bar. He had a red sleeveless flannel shirt and huge muscles. His hair was long and slicked back looking like a reddish-brown and he was sporting a thick beard. His arms were covered in tattoos. When she looked at his face and those deadly looking eyes, her heart felt like it stopped beating. She knew that look. That was the look of a man who had seen horrible things. The eyes of a killer.

She quickly lowered her eyes but then Clover was pulling her toward the man.

"Thermo, I'd like for you to meet Kai. She's the one I told you about. The one who helped Felix. Kai, meet Thermo Stelling."

When he stood up from the stool, he looked her over and she swore she felt his eyes touch her body. The man was huge, way over six feet tall, and she was shaking as he reached his hand out to shake hers. When their fingers touched, she practically gasped. What the hell was wrong with her tonight? Three good looking guys in a row she never met before shake her hand hello and she feels so much so soon. She pulled back and looked at Clover, then back at Thermo. *Did he say Stelling?*

"Stelling? Wait are you related to Selasi and Zayn?" she asked him, and he squinted at her.

"You know my brothers?" he asked, and again looked her over from head to toe, and holy shit she felt aroused.

Her cheeks warmed and then she heard Clover say something to someone behind him, leaving her talking to Thermo all by herself. "I just met them a few minutes ago. I'm good friends with Afina and Mike."

"Really? I never saw you around before."

"I don't really come out too much. I work a lot."

"Hmm," he said in a mumble, with those deadly eyes of his.

She squinted at him. "So, you know Felix?" She wondered why she was even trying to keep a conversation with the man when he seemed like he didn't like talking, and honestly looked mean.

"Known him for years. We were in boot camp together."

"So you're in the military?" Kai got that instant sensation like an alert that it didn't matter she felt attracted to the man, he was military and she was staying clear from military and law enforcement. Maybe silly, but it kept her in a place where she wouldn't have to face her fears or the sadness of losing Edison.

"I'm retired now. As of two years ago," he said to her.

"What do you do now to keep busy?"

He just stared at her. She felt completely uncomfortable. Was he staring at her wondering why she was still here talking to him, or was he staring at her because he was checking her out? Did she care?

"I mean, you don't have to be doing anything, but I understand from talking to a lot of soldiers that it's hard for them not to keep busy and active in something. Just figured I would ask."

"I do a lot of different things."

Man, it was like pulling teeth. Why was she still standing there?

"What about you? Clover and Ghost mentioned a young woman who had gotten multiple programs together to help soldiers and first responders. Do you come from a family of them?"

"My brother was a State Trooper back in New Jersey."

"Oh, a Jersey girl, huh? How come no accent?" he asked.

She smirked. Was he being funny? So odd. The man definitely didn't look like he had a sense of humor. He was serious and hard-core. Definitely. "I guess I lost it over the years being down south. Maybe I have a little bit of a weird accent now. You know a combination of New Jersey and Southern drawl?" she said, and then licked her lower lip.

"You have a nice tone of voice. Soft and quiet. I can barely hear you."

Just then some guys pressed in behind her to order drinks at the bar. She looked over her shoulder.

"Kai? Hey, what are you doing here?" one of the guys asked.

She knew him form the hospital. He worked with some of the amputees with rehabilitation. He hugged her hello and then he looked at Thermo who stepped back, as if he didn't want to be introduced.

"I'm here with friends."

"Let me buy you a drink," he said.

"That's okay. I have one." He looked disappointed. "Maybe later."

"Okay, I'll hold you to that." He winked and then she turned back toward Thermo, but now Zayn was there.

"You met my brother?" he asked her.

She gave a soft smile. "Clover introduced me to him. I should head back to Afina and Mike."

Zayn placed his hand on her hip and moved her so she was away from the guys at the bar and now between him and Thermo. "Stay so we can talk. I want to hear more about this organization you have developed and the programs being offered," Zayn said.

"Programs?" Thermo asked.

Kai began to explain about the organization and before long she talked about how things got started, all the different people in the community who were helping out, and about meeting so many people and truly hoping to serve even more soldiers and first responders in the next year.

She took a sip of the new rum and soda Thermo had gotten her, and Zayn started talking about how long they knew Mike and some of the crazy things he used to do.

"How about you guys? Special Forces are pretty intense. Takes a superior kind of soldier to make it through the training never mind missions," she said to them.

"I suppose in your line of work you meet a lot of soldiers?" Zayn asked, and looked at her in a way that made her feel like maybe he thought she hooked up with soldiers. She wanted to laugh. She stayed clear of men, period.

"You learn about the different ranks of each branch, although some Seals think they have Special Forces beat, never mind Green Berets," she said, egging them on.

"Bullshit. I can guarantee we're better," Zayn said, and slid his hand along her waist, giving her hip a squeeze. She stared up at him and into those dark eyes of his. Thank God he was so much taller or she would fear the man might lean down and kiss her. With that thought she panicked and stepped away, only to bump into Thermo's thigh.

"Are you going to Mike's place tomorrow for the barbecue he's throwing?" Zayn asked as he nonchalantly placed his hand on the bar next to her side.

"I didn't get invited," she said.

"Oh, I'm sure you're invited. Mike couldn't stop talking about you."

"What?"

"Oh yeah, we heard some stories about your college days and when Mike visited Afina," Zayn told her.

"Were you a wild thing in college?" Thermo asked, still no real facial expression. Just cold, dark, mysterious to someone unknown to military men who experienced war. She knew though, and she wasn't interested in any games they were playing.

"Well, I'm sure he told you I had a boyfriend through college."

"He did. A soldier, right?" Zayn asked.

She felt the tears reach her eyes and turned away.

Zayn's hand went to her shoulder and he squeezed it. "It isn't easy dating a soldier, especially active duty and a Marine," Zayn said to her.

"I'd rather not talk about it. In fact. I think I'm going to go join my friends. It was nice meeting you, Thermo. Enjoy the evening." She put her drink down.

Zayn pulled her close and whispered into her ear. "I wish you would stay and talk. You're so easy to talk to."

She closed her eyes and willed the attraction away. It wasn't right. She promised to never love again. To focus on saving lives and not getting caught up in the drama and the fears.

"I'm not interested, Zayn. There are plenty of other women around here that would love to talk to you and your brother. Have a good night." She pushed away from him and walked away. What she hadn't expected was to feel guilty and disappointed. Where did these men come from? Maybe it was time to call it a night.

* * * *

"What did you say to scare her away?" Selasi asked, passing by Kai as she walked away. His brother smiled and winked, but Kai kept walking. Zayn wondered why.

"He was pushy," Thermo said, and then reached for a bottle of Bud Light and took a sip, his eyes on both Selasi and Zayn.

"She's so beautiful. I don't think I have ever met a woman with eyes like hers," Zayn said. He couldn't believe how attracted to her he was. It was instant, too. That long reddish-brown hair that cascaded down her back and over her shoulders in abundant curls. Then the color of her eyes, so blue, and enhanced by her thick eyelashes and perfect face. Her skin was flawless, and she smelled so good. Holy crap he was fantasizing about the woman. Still thinking about her even though she wasn't right here. She basically blew him and his brothers off. His brothers. He looked at Selasi and Thermo.

"You think she's hot? You felt an attraction?" he asked both of them.

"Every fucking guy in this place would find her attractive, Zayn," Selasi said, and then took a slug of beer from the bottle he held.

"No. That isn't what I mean," Zayn said, and looked around the place in search of Kai again. His brothers remained silent. Zayn was interested in Kai and instead of telling his brothers his plan, he held it inside and hoped she would show up at the barbeque tomorrow.

Chapter Four

Amelia was walking down the street a block from her house when she heard her cell phone ring. She hoped that it wasn't Afina and the girls again trying to get her to show up at the barbecue at Mike's place. She wasn't really in the mood to socialize, and was feeling so burnt out and frustrated about breaking up with Cavanaugh. Her head was fuzzy and nothing was really worth focusing on. She pulled her cell phone out of her bag and answered it. "Hello?"

"Hey, baby."

She gasped. Her heart felt as if it stopped beating. Why was he calling her? What did he want? She was so damn scared of him. Afraid of his fierce temper and of course his hard hands.

"Talk to me. I miss you, honey. I want to see you."

"No," she said, but her voice cracked, the emotion, the fear obvious and he knew it. She could see that smug expression, the way he would know she was scared of him and anything he said or did to her lasted hours, even days. He was a monster.

"Don't...don't say no. I know you miss me." He started the sentence so fierily, she thought for sure that he would start yelling, but he didn't. It was like the last several arguments they had over the phone where he couldn't reach out, grab her by her hair, or her neck under her hair and press her to him as he whispered harshly against her ear. She shivered, but she didn't hang up. She couldn't hang up. She feared him and her body began to shake.

"I don't want any trouble, Cavanaugh."

"Then meet me. Invite me over. Let's talk."

"I'm not talking to you. You don't know how to talk, only use your power."

"I'm getting tired of this shit, Amelia. Tired of these fucking games. So I hit you. Get over it. You should know better than to flirt with those soldiers that come into that place."

"I wasn't flirting with anyone."

"Bullshit!!" He screamed into the phone and she panicked. She ended the call and then regretted it. The old familiar sensations invaded her mind and she started to cry. She placed her hand over her heart and felt the panic attack begin. She was so fucked up. So screwed because of this man and his abuse. She sat in an office that helped people get over fears, anxiety, stress, and yet here she was drowning in her fears. Scared to even go out at night because Cavanaugh could be waiting for her.

Would he go that far? He left her alone all week. She started to pace her apartment. Should she call the police? Call Kai or Afina? God, Afina will tell her to come over. Hell, she would send Mike or one of the guys. God forbid she sent Fogerty. Oh God.

She thought of him. A mercenary. A gorgeous, rugged, intimidating man who was mysterious and was the center of her fantasies. A fantasy she held on to and needed to get over Cavanaugh. To try and put the fears Cavanaugh placed in her behind her, but that was all it was. She would be so embarrassed if Fogerty knew she was abused by her boyfriend and was weak, easily manipulated and so much more. Maybe she needed to consider leaving Mercy, hell leave South Carolina entirely.

More tears flowed and she went toward the window. She was on the fourth floor and she peaked outside. She looked for Cavanaugh's blue pickup truck. She knew the sound of the diesel engine and the way the muffler rattled so it made a cool sound. She used to think he was amazing. No, he was a monster. Her cell phone rang but this time she didn't answer it. Instead she ignored it and cried. She wasn't going anywhere tonight. She was staying home, with the door locked, and the phone and bat by her bed.

Please don't let him come here tonight. Please keep him away from me. Please.

* * * *

"You're still coming over, right?" Afina asked Kai. Kai exhaled and Afina whined over the phone. "Come on, please. You can't leave me with all these damn men. I'll go out of my mind. I need reinforcements. You, Sally, Mel, and Amelia, although she might be a no-show. I called her twice and texted several times and she said she had a bad headache."

"So maybe she does."

"Well, you come over, and bring that special guacamole dip you make so well."

Kai chuckled. I'm not sure it's a good idea."

"Why the hell not?"

"Uhmm, I don't know."

"Oh…so Mike was right. Holy shit. You sure do know how to pick men to get back into the dating scene with."

"What?"

Afina chuckled. "Don't "what" me girl. I saw your eyes widen at the sight of Zayn. He is gorgeous, and then Selasi and Thermo. Hell, Thermo doesn't react or talk to anyone. They couldn't take their eyes off of you either."

"Oh no. Then I am definitely not coming over."

"You have to."

"I don't have to do anything. I'm perfectly fine not placing myself into an uncomfortable situation."

"Sweetie, those men are gorgeous, and so damn intimidating, of course you're a chicken."

"A chicken? Afina?" Kai scolded her.

Afina laughed. "I get your fears, honey, but I have to say I have never seen you look at any man who has tried hitting on you the way you looked at them. I think they were affected by you, as well."

"I'm not interested in dating anyone or entertaining some little attraction. Of course any woman would feel aroused by them and their good looks and bodies."

"Aroused? Oh wow, you really do like them. This is so awesome."

"No, not awesome."

"Yes, completely."

"I'm not coming over."

"Yes, you are. Be here by two, and don't forget the guac!"

* * * *

"I'm at my wit's end, Chadwick. My brother and his wife have tried everything. It's one of those tough cases. The kind that no one seems to be able to handle."

"I understand, John. I do, but have you reached out to Guardians Hope?" Chadwick asked, instantly thinking of Kai Devaro as he held the phone to his ear. She was truly an amazing woman and dedicated to helping soldiers like Kenny.

"I have, Chadwick. Kenny was seeing someone there and then he stopped going, and started to become irate again. He can get violent. My sister in law has suffered his wrath before. My brother and his wife don't want to kick him out but it is getting to be too much. They have concerns for their own children."

"Understandable. He needs more help, perhaps medical first, to help deal with the anger issues."

"They come out of nowhere. He can be perfectly calm and then suddenly he snaps. He was doing well for months. We just don't understand why he snapped."

"Well, why don't I give my friend a call? She created Guardians Angels. She knows not only what to do for Kenny, but she'll help get things moving quickly."

"Thank you so much. My brother and his wife will be relieved."

"I'll be in touch," Chadwick said, and then ended the call.

He looked up at the clock. It was four in the afternoon on a Saturday, but Kai wouldn't mind. She had a huge heart.

* * * *

"I'm so glad you came. See, it isn't so bad, and I caught you checking out Zayn before when he wasn't looking," Afina said to Kai.

Kai pushed her hair to one side and she shook her head. "I wasn't staring."

"Honey, you are interested and I think it's great. Why are you fighting it?"

"Afina, we've been over this before. I'm not interested in dating anyone, getting close to anyone or taking any chances on one man never mind multiple, and...never mind military and police."

"That's stupid, and you're good with men like that. You understand their stresses and the pressure they are under. I think it is inevitable. You'll wind up falling in love with a soldier, a cop, or close to it. I guarantee it."

"Love again? Never," she said, and then her cell phone rang. Afina took a sip of her tropical drink as Kai glanced at her cell phone.

"Who is it?"

"Chadwick." She excused herself just as Zayn and Mike were approaching.

"Who is that?" Mike asked.

"Dr. Hayes," Afina said, and Mike made a noise but Kai walked away from them to answer the call.

"Hello, Chadwick, how are you?" she asked, walking toward the far patio and a bench that was there. No one was over there right now so she had some privacy.

"Hello, Kai, so nice to hear your voice. I'm not bothering you, am I?" he asked in that very distinguished, almost arrogant tone. He spoke with his nose sort of in the air but not really. It was hard to describe. He could be a bit arrogant, but he was the top emergency surgeon in the United States so why not?

"I'm just at a friend's house for a barbecue."

"How nice. I won't keep you long. I have a friend who needs some guidance for his nephew. Perhaps we can meet up tomorrow and talk about it?"

"I have plans tomorrow with Canton and the family. Maybe I can call you if I get back early enough."

"You're so busy. No wonder we can never coordinate a dinner date."

"Chadwick."

"I know, you don't date, but I was hoping to change your mind. We'd be good together."

"There is more to a relationship than the public's perception of it," she replied.

"True, but my attraction to you goes beyond image."

She didn't know what to say. He was being very forward and she didn't have the same feelings for him.

"I've silenced you and that isn't my intention. Call me when you have a chance to talk. This soldier needs services. He walked out on the therapist several times at Guardians Hope."

"So he is already in the system with us?" she asked, her care for this unknown soldier immediate. These were the ones who needed the most help before it was too late. She pushed for more information and he explained a bit.

"I will get the ball rolling. See if his parents can get him to attend the session on Tuesday. I'll do what I can."

"You mean you'll show up and help him personally?"

"I'll try. Hopefully I can convince him that he needs the help he does."

"You're an angel, Kai."

She needed the call a few seconds later and then placed her hands on the stone wall and looked out toward the yard. She could hear music and laughter behind her, but her focus always went back to that lonely feeling in her gut. The emptiness from losing Edison.

"Important phone call?" She gasped and turned to see Zayn standing there holding two drinks. A tropical one and a bottle of Bud Light.

"Sort of." She gave a soft smile.

"Here, Afina sent me over with it." He handed her the glass and she took it. "To making new friends," he said, and they clinked glasses.

She couldn't help but to take in his features, and find him completely attractive, sexy, and everything a man should be. She didn't want to compare him to Edison. They were different, all men were, but the things she found attractive about Zayn were different than Edison. Of course looks were initially what drew her in, but it was Zayn's eyes, that rugged look about him, yet his beard was well trimmed and short, unlike Thermo's.

She stopped herself. What the hell was she thinking? She turned to look back toward the yard.

"They have a nice place," Zayn said, and she felt him step closer.

"They sure do. I don't know how they leave it," she said to him.

"I'm sure it's tough when they have to go, but they probably focus on returning. I definitely don't miss any of that."

She glanced over her shoulder at him, then turned toward him as she leaned against the stone wall. "You miss it?"

He stepped closer and held her gaze. "I miss some parts of it. The camaraderie, the danger, helping other friends and being a part of something so great and patriotic."

"That's understandable. I'm sure it's difficult to transition back into civilian life, but you seem to be doing fine."

"I'm doing great and so are my brothers. It took some time to get used to things. We don't slack in anything really."

She took a sip of her drink and stared up into his dark blue eyes.

"Like what?"

"Making the beds, keeping the house clean, organizing responsibilities around the house and at work. Our jobs still incorporate our training and our experiences."

"Do you think that's important when trying to get back into a routine as a civilian? Finding a job, or responsibility that incorporates the training and discipline? Like maybe it's necessary to survive?"

He stared at her. "You're always thinking, aren't you? About ways to help soldiers heal?"

She felt a little embarrassed. She didn't mean to ask questions like she was analyzing him. She tightened up when she felt his fingers under her chin. He was in front of her now and she just stared up at him, shocked at the attraction she felt.

"You're so damn beautiful."

"Zayn," she said his name and went to turn, but he cupped her cheek, stepping even closer to her.

"I know you feel the attraction."

He released her cheek and lowered his hand to her hip. "Talk to me. I want to get to know you."

"As friends, Zayn, that's fine."

She could feel him stroking her hip, and then his fingers grazed under her top to her skin. Her lips parted. She gasped.

"You feel it. Don't be afraid of me."

As she looked at him and imagined being held by Zayn, kissed by Zayn, she panicked. She pressed away, nearly spilling her drink.

"Is it the doctor? The guy you were just talking to? The one who wants you in his bed?" he asked her and she was shocked.

She squinted at him.

"What?"

"Afina said the doctor wants you in his bed."

"Afina has a big mouth. She shouldn't say things like that, and no, it isn't the doctor, Zayn. It's me." She felt the tears fill her eyes. She took a deep breath and he took her hand. He brought it to his lips and softly kissed her knuckles.

"I'm willing to wait. To take my time and go slow if that's what you need. If you aren't attracted to me, because you're so gorgeous and can get any guy you want, so why pick one like me, I get it."

She was surprised by his words. She put her drink down and then reached for his arm. "No. No, Zayn, that isn't it at all. I...I'm incapable of opening up my heart to another man."

He shook his head, brought her hand to his chest and reached out and stroked her hair as he shook his head. "You're just scared. I get it. Let's just hang out and be friends for now. Whatever happens, happens."

She was relieved that he didn't push for more. Yet part of her felt like she could tell him why she wouldn't accept his advances. Then of course there was the part of her that wanted to feel him close, feel Zayn's lips against hers. She needed to slow things down. Then she heard Selasi's voice as he joined them.

"What do we have going on over here, a private party?" he asked.

"No, I was just talking Kai into a game of pool."

"Pool, huh? I want in on this. We doing partners or one on one?" he asked, and looked her over. Selasi was definitely a flirt.

"One on one. I don't know how good Kai is," Zayn said.

She took her glass and the three of them headed back toward the house and to the game room off the patio by the pool. In all of about fifteen minutes later, she was laughing and enjoying the conversation with them as well as Devin and their friends who teased one another. She was also kicking Zayn's butt in pool.

* * * *

Thermo watched Kai playing pool with everyone. The woman was gorgeous with her long reddish blonde hair, her sexy figure, especially the way her ass looked in the tight dark jeans she wore and that top. God damn, every time she bent down to take a shot on the pool table her blouse gaped open and he could see the deep cleavage of her abundant breasts. Her laugh was addicting, too. She had a funny laugh that was contagious.

He sipped at his beer and didn't understand how he could be affected by this woman. It was more than just her physical appearance and beauty, it was her soft tone of voice, her calming demeanor, and the way she gave her full attention to whomever she spoke to. She dressed classy, even now in designer jeans, a pretty pale cream blouse and camisole that matched. She also wore wedge sandals that made her thighs look sexy and long. He was pretty surprised by his attraction to her, considering he hardly spoke to her. Then of course, knowing that Zayn and Selasi already liked her and found her attractive, too, made him think of things they talked about while serving.

Relationships, feeling venerable or weak in certain areas. Hell, he was the weakest link. He was the fucked up one. He didn't like to be touched. Kept people away. Didn't want a woman seeing his scars, the damage from his last fucking mission that should have ended his life. He didn't want to come across fucked up, but he was. He knew it. He had nightmares. He woke up with tears spilling from his eyes several times as he remembered his fallen brothers-in-arms. How badly they were tortured before they died. He did things most human beings couldn't understand or even begin to understand. He killed, and killed, and killed some more, until killing didn't give him that sick, bad feeling in his gut. He became desensitized to life, because the reality was kill or get killed.

He looked around at their friends, at Devin who just wrapped his arms around Kai's waist and hugged her tight as she laughed, and he wondered why he lived and why others died? What was he supposed to do with this life, when nothing seemed to get to him, or make him feel?

His eyes roamed over Kai once again and this time it was Mike keeping his hand on her hip and talking to Turner and Fogerty, Watson, Dell, and Phantom, all mercenaries, all soldiers who now used their killing skills and military abilities to make money. She deserved men who were whole. Men like his brothers Selasi who was using his military skills to train police officers and special units. A man like Zayn who was hired by the state police as a trainer for undercover investigators like Devin. Guys who used their abilities to help others. Thermo felt alone and useless. Except maybe to spar with and help train some of these men who were going to see hand-to-hand combat at any point in their professions. Otherwise, he had nothing. Except those thoughts, those nightmares of his past.

* * * *

Kai looked at Devin's eye and then his cheek. She stroked his jaw. "I don't like seeing this," she said to him in front of Selasi, Mike, and Turner.

Devin wrapped his arm around her waist and gave her hip a squeeze. "I'm fine, Kai. You don't need to worry about me."

"I do though. You take too many chances. You need to be more careful."

"I am careful. It's the criminals that are getting worse."

"In his defense, I hear the guys and Zayn all the time talking about how issuing warrants in some of these places is not a walk in the park anymore," Selasi said to her.

"Add in the disrespect for law enforcement and of course they're going to resist," Turner stated.

"What happened this time?" Afina asked, joining the conversation.

"We went in, but before we made it to the apartment we were stopped by a few guys asking us questions, like we have to give them answers. That was bullshit right there," Devin said.

"So they were the ones that attacked you?" Kai asked.

"Pretty much. They shoved us and we shoved back, and were prepared to draw our weapons when this guy punches me in the eye. I hit him back and he goes down, and my partner is grabbing the other one when he throws a right hook at my cheek. It was a freaking mess," Devin said.

"So what about the guy you came to arrest?" Kai asked.

"We got him while he was sneaking down the hallway. Turns out those guys were there to distract us. Didn't work, but I wound up with this," Devin said.

Kai shook her head and then stepped to the side as Turner gave him a pretend shot, which Devin blocked.

"You were doing all right with the ladies last night," Mike teased.

"Yes I was," he said, and then took a slug from his bottle of Bud Light.

"You better be careful, Devin. There are some crazy stalker women sniffing around you lately. I hope you didn't hook up with any last night," Afina teased.

"What? Like who?" Devin asked.

"Oh I don't know, maybe that little blonde who was rubbing your thigh and whispering in your ear," Afina teased once again.

"A stalker? Shit, there are plenty of those around Corporals. A lot of women go there to hook up and fulfill their little fantasies about doing a soldier," Turner said, and then took a slug from his beer bottle.

Devin snickered. "Not for nothing, but I think any of us could handle a stalker."

"She would have to be really good in—"

Afina covered Devin's mouth and everyone started laughing.

Kai felt the hand on her hip as Selasi squeezed next to her. The man was so big and tall. She felt like a peanut compared to him. His hand was huge, too, and could cover her hip. His fingers thick and long, felt like they were burning her skin through her jeans.

"Now you know one of the reasons why my brothers and I don't go there much. Damn glad we were there last night though to meet you," he whispered.

"Selasi, I told Zayn I'm not—"

"I get it. I can go slow, sweetie," he said as he held her gaze and gave her a wink. However, his eyes roamed to her lips and she wondered how it would feel to have him kiss her.

She was feeling pretty damn confused. Two brothers? Two retired soldiers and one heavily involved in dangerous police work, and she was attracted to them? Then there was Thermo who hadn't said a word to her tonight at all. He sat there in the corner, quiet, barely exchanging words with the other men. Why she thought of the three of them as a package made her heart race. Was she thinking about a ménage? Surely this was just physical, a need for sex. Sex she hadn't had in more than three years, or been held close to just snuggle, or have the security of a muscular man's arms like she had with Edison.

She felt the hand against her cheek and snapped out of her thoughts.

"Damn, baby, what were you just thinking? You looked so sad, so lost," he said to her, and she realized that everyone got quiet around her.

She glanced that way and Turner, Mike, Devin, Afina, and Zayn stared at her. "I'm fine. Excuse me please." She stepped away from him.

"Kai." He said her name and she shook her head and forced a smile.

"I'm good, Selasi," she said, and headed inside.

Kai walked down the hallway and went into the extra sitting room. She looked out the window at the evening stars and thought about Edison. The tears filled her eyes, and she tried to keep them away. She missed him but things were changing. After years of being lonely and forcing herself to just live each day alone and strong, here she was having feelings for other men. Why did she feel so guilty, and also so scared?

She gasped when she felt the hand on her waist. *Michael.*

"It's okay, Kai. You're an amazing, sexy, hot, gorgeous, young woman with one hell of a body, plus brains, so you knew this was going to happen." She laughed but tears fell. He hugged her tight from behind and placed his chin on her shoulder.

"I'll be okay."

"You will be with men as awesome as those three."

"Three?" she asked and turned, looking up at him with tears in her eyes. He smiled softly and stroked the tear from her cheek.

"You've never reacted to any men like you have with those three. We all can see it plain as day. Hell, I'm jealous." He winked.

She knew he was teasing. She and Mike had that kind of fun relationship where he always joked about taking her to bed to be friends with benefits. She stared at him. "I'm not ready."

"Sure you are."

"No. I'm shaking. Can't you feel it?" she whispered.

"Even if you didn't have the sadness of the past, and I know I don't have all the details, I think most people react with a bit of fear when they get struck with being attracted to someone again, and they know it's more than just physical."

"How can you say that when you haven't had one serious relationship since I've known you?"

"I'm a man, Kai. I got needs and shit, but I know the difference between sex and a one-night stand and something more. I just haven't met anyone like that yet, nor has my team."

"Your team? You mean you and the whole crew with one woman? A ménage? You want that?"

"Come here." He took her hand and brought her over to the couch. They sat down and she turned sideways, crossed her legs, and listened to him. "Phantom, Turner, and I have been teamed up in the military for years. A shit load of our friends have engaged in ménage relationships for a lot of reasons, but the most common ones make sense."

"Like?"

He took a deep breath and released it. "Like knowing if one of us can't handle something, that the others can. That a woman, our woman, will be kept safe at all times because at least one of us can be with her if not all three. Soldiers who have experienced and seen violence and shit like we all have, need to know that our mate, our woman is safe. I know you may not understand—"

She shook her head and reached out and covered his forearm. "I understand. Without getting into details, I understand." She thought about the things Edison said to her when he was struggling so much once he was back home. He kept asking about his friends, the rest of his troop, the four guys he thought of as brothers, but they were dead. He survived and they died. Tears spilled from her eyes. He squinted at her.

"You do understand," he said, but was shocked.

She tried to talk to him about Edison but she couldn't.

"It's okay. You don't need to explain. There's a lot of benefits to a ménage and I think it might be a good fit for you, besides the fact that I don't think one man could handle you."

"What is that supposed to mean?" she asked and wiped her eyes.

He looked her over and smiled. "You're an idiot."

"But you love me like a brother, right?"

"Right," she said, and he hugged her. "Take your time, and if you want any dirt on those three just ask, but they're good men. Hard men but loyal and trustworthy."

"We'll see," she said, and he pulled back.

"Now, back to the party?"

She looked at her watch, and he grabbed her hand and pulled her from the couch, turning her toward the doorway. "Don't even think about heading out." He gave her ass a slap.

She gasped. "Mike!"

"It's probably the last time I get to do that." He winked and then nodded his head toward the right. There stood Selasi and Zayn by themselves near the pool table. She released Mike's hand, but then North saw her.

"Kai, come here. You have to see this," she said, and Kai noticed how Mike looked at North, but North was sitting with a few of their other friends, some troopers in the same unit as Devin, and he didn't look happy. Could Mike have his eyes on North?

Kai walked over and said hello to the guys. Some she knew by face and others not at all. They looked at this crazy video on television with people doing off the wall stunts. One scene after the next was funny and had them all laughing. She knew immediately when Selasi and Zayn were right behind her, and she didn't panic. She tried to just let things happen. When both men pressed close and she could feel them inhale against her hair, and then both of them touch her, she closed her eyes and just breathed through it. She stared at the television as she absorbed the sensation of their large hands against her skin. Selasi's on her lower back, caressing her and Zayn's on her shoulder, then under her neck in such a sexual, dominating way. She tried not to think about intimacy, about sex, but it was hard as her body responded, making her realize that she had fought against any sensations of desire for so long, even the slight attraction to a man, but that this felt different. She didn't turn to look at them or catch their eyes, she just pretended to focus on the television and the funny scenes as others laughed, until her eyes moved from the television toward the opened doors and patio to where Thermo was in a dead stare at her. She didn't turn away and neither did he. Something clicked. She liked them, and was attracted to the three men. Now what?

* * * *

Selasi and Zayn kept Kai close to them and she wasn't pulling away. He didn't know what Mike and her had talked about earlier, but whatever it was seemed to help her relax a little. He wanted to make plans with her, but was it moving too fast? He wondered, but then Zayn asked.

"How about we try to get together for lunch or dinner this week?"

She looked up at Zayn and she swallowed hard. "I have a busy schedule. I heard you mentioning you're pretty busy, too."

"We could rearrange some things. Or how about tomorrow?"

"Oh, I have plans with friends tomorrow that I haven't seen in a while. This week is going to be a bit crazy, and Friday night I have a banquet to attend."

"A banquet for what?" Selasi asked, not hiding his upset at her declining a date.

"The Mercy Community Council awards ceremony. Black tie affair at the Silvermore on the water front."

"Impressive place. That's by invitation only, right?" Zayn asked, staring at her lips.

"It is and was planned for months. I'm going to support a few friends who are receiving awards who have been great contributors to Guardians Hope. I'm also representing the charity and hoping to receive some more donations to the latest projects we're developing."

"What are the new projects?" Selasi asked. He loved the tone of her voice. It was soft, sweet, and a little raspy, making her come off even sexier than she already was.

"Currently, we just broke ground on a retreat center where soldiers or law enforcement officers suffering from PTSD or other disorders can go for private counseling and recreation. A calm, non-intrusive, non hospital setting, where they feel more relaxed and at ease. We also have established a car service with all volunteers to help transport soldiers or first responders that need transportation to and from the medical facilities. Some have to travel weekly for chemo treatments or same day surgical procedures and even counseling, but they don't have driver's licenses and the cost of car service is too much. Taking a bus can be too costly or even take too long with stops, and if they are sensitive to certain environmental factors it could add to their stresses. We're trying to think of all the different ways we can serve our heroes and make them know how appreciative we are and return the favor of their sacrifices. It's coming along pretty good so far." She went on about it, and he just was more and more impressed with her.

"That's awesome, Kai. I love all those ideas and it's amazing to learn that you're making them happen," Zayn said, and covered her hand with his.

She smiled softly. "Not me alone. Believe me it has taken years, but it's well worth it."

"What's your ultimate goal? What will make you feel like you've achieved it all?" Selasi asked.

She was quiet a moment and then pulled her hand back and looked at them. "To make the percentage of suicides by soldiers and first responders nonexistent. To reach every single one of them, and make them feel they aren't alone, that we have their backs," she said, and then took her drink and swallowed.

He was shocked, but before he could say a word, her friends interrupted and no plans were made, but he was going to find a way to make some with her. He wanted to learn more about Kai Devaro.

Chapter Five

"You were really quiet at Mike's last night. I only saw you talking to Kai a little bit. Don't you like her?" Zayn asked Thermo.

He just stared at Zayn.

"What?" Zayn asked.

Thermo leaned forward by the table. He had some things packed to head to his friend's house. He hadn't seen Keono for months, and now they ran some martial arts classes together training soldiers and law enforcement officers.

"You think she wants to date a soldier and a cop when you heard she lost her brother who was a cop, and her boyfriend who committed suicide and was a soldier? She's scared of us. Of what we stand for. Selasi and I as soldiers and you as a soldier and law enforcement."

"She feels the attraction like we all do. She's just scared and I get it. It's a lot to take in, I know, but she would understand who we are and what we need and require in a woman."

"We?"

"Fuck yeah, you, too. You're not running from this, Thermo. You like her. I've never seen you look at a woman like you look at Kai," Selasi added, joining them in the kitchen.

"First, she's fucking hot, second, it doesn't bother you that all the guys hit on her, and they even touch her, pull her into their arms and shit."

"You mean Mike and Devin, Turner and Fogerty? Hell, they've known her for years. She isn't interested in any of them," Selasi said.

"Definitely not interested. Mike can be relentless when he sets his sights on a woman. If it's true and he has hit on her for years and she hasn't taken him up on it, then it will never happen," Zayn said.

"Definitely not happen if we make a move together," Selasi said.

"I'm not ready for anything more," Thermo added.

"We've talked about this. About our insecurities and where we lack, where we need one another as reinforcement and support. A ménage, us sharing one woman together, loving her, providing for her together would be perfect for the three of us," Zayn said to him.

"You guys have your shit together. You can flirt, you can function. I close up. I'm fine being silent, and considering what she does for a living, you can't tell me she isn't going to force me to talk."

"You're scared of trusting her?" Selasi asked.

"I trust the two of you."

"Then trust that she's the one. I'm telling you, no other woman has given me these feelings and has made me feel like this. None. I say we take the fucking chance, and if it doesn't work out, then it doesn't. We won't know unless we take the risk," Zayn replied.

"I just don't know if this is right. I don't know if I can give her anything. I still have nightmares and shit. Things set me off."

"You have control over that though and you don't lose it. She won't be scared of you or a situation," Zayn said to him.

"How do you know, man? What if we're in bed together and I wake up not knowing where the fuck I am? I could hurt her, hell crush her. She's like five-feet-five. We're over six-feet-three, and more than a hundred and eighty pounds heavier, never mind my capabilities."

"Another reason why sharing her, taking her together, protects her," Selasi told him.

"I'm just not sure. You guys go ahead, but I need time still. I just don't know."

Thermo got up and grabbed his bag. "I'll be back late."

Zayn nodded. "Tell Keono and the family hello for us."

"Will do."

* * * *

Thermo headed out, his heart heavy and his mind on the situation and on the past. He very well could have been a part of that statistic of suicides by soldiers when he returned from Baghdad Soldiers just didn't talk about their feelings and emotions. They kept that shit all bottled up inside and then exploded. Some more often than others, and some just waited and waited until it was all too much, and in a fit of fear and frustration they felt there was nowhere else to turn but to end their lives.

When he got to the Shaden estate, where Keono lived in a separate house on his family's property, he was surprised to see the white jeep in the driveway. He was pretty sure that Kai had a white jeep, but how would she know the Shadens? Canton Shaden, Keono's father was a business tycoon and filthy rich. It had to be a coincidence.

He parked the truck and then grabbed his bag looking forward to doing some sparring with Keono in the home gym before relaxing by poolside or in the Jacuzzi just shooting the shit. He rang the door and Canton answered it.

"Thermo. Good to see you. Come on in," he said, inviting him into their very upscale, classy home. The formal living room to the right contained a large family portrait. They had four sons, but one son, Leon, was a soldier who had committed suicide. Two other sons were involved in law enforcement after the military and Keono hadn't taken on another career after retiring from the service. When Thermo and his brothers moved back into Mercy, Keono found out and looked him up. It was about a year ago.

"Thermo, how are you?" Mrs. Shaden greeted him. She didn't approach to hug him, knowing that he wasn't an affectionate man. That was another indicator why he wasn't ready for a relationship with a woman.

"Keono is out back in the dojo. Why don't you head out there, and when you all are done we have plenty of food and drinks so you can relax by poolside. It's a hot one today," Canton said to him.

"Thanks a lot. I'll see you in a little bit," he said, and then headed out the side door, down the walkway, and to the private house with the additional building next to it that Keono turned into a dojo.

The closer he got the more he realized that Keono was sparring with someone. When he opened the door he could see Keono and someone else all decked out in fighting protective gear on their heads. The other person he sparred shot a kick up into his head. Keono stepped back and then countered the next move, the two of them going at it pretty intensely. He squinted as he caught a slight bit of reddish-brown hair peeking out of the top part of the headgear, and as she turned she paused and Keono knocked her onto her ass.

"Keono!" she yelled at him, her voice raspy and so not forceful sounding, and he knew it was Kai.

"You weren't paying attention. Too busy looking at Thermo. He has that effect on women but he never seems to react to any," Keono said, and reached down to give her a hand but she jumped up from her position with no hands and did a move on Keono, sending him onto his ass.

Thermo watched in amusement and a bit of jealousy as Keono scrambled across the mat to grab her ankle and pull her down, and then two of then rolled around on the mats, doing moves until she was on top of him.

"Okay, I don't need my nose broken by you again. I give," Keono said, and Kai laughed.

She shoved at his shoulder. "You don't ever give up. Now no more sneaky moves. I want to say hello to Thermo," she said, and stood up.

Keono did, too, and they both took off the headgear. Kai's face was flushed, her blue eyes sparkled, and her hair was all pulled back tight and in some sort of ball at the base of her head.

"What are you doing here? How do you know Kai?" he asked.

"Oh shit, Kai, this is one of the guys you were talking to me about?" Keono asked, looking shocked.

But Thermo found the information positive, and he looked her over. "Talking about me behind my back?" he asked in a harsh tone.

"I mentioned the party and a few things," she replied, and then walked to the side to take a sip from a bottle of water.

"This is awesome," Keono said, and then shook Thermo's hand.

"We need to talk, but first, let's do some sparring. We can both show Kai some moves, if you let me touch her I mean," he teased.

Thermo raised one eyebrow up at him, and considering Thermo was six inches taller, Keono raised his hands up.

"Let's do it, then we can go swimming and relax by the pool."

Thermo brought his bag to the bench where Kai sat watching them. He stared at her a moment and she stared at him.

"You looked good out there. I bet you could handle Zayn's class he does at the dojo."

"Oh she definitely can handle that class. But the guys you all train might be intimidated by her. She gets fierce," Keono said, and smiled at her.

"You're a good teacher, Keono."

"How did you two meet anyway?" Thermo asked, joining Keono on the mats.

"She's my guardian angel." Keono winked.

Before Thermo could ask more, Keono took a shot at him and their sparring session began.

* * * *

What were the chances that Thermo was the good friend, a fellow soldier Keono knew from basic training? Keno never mentioned him until today and even then, he didn't say his name. She was a little embarrassed that Keono mentioned her telling him about Thermo and his brothers, but her and Keono became friends over the last three years, since she met his father who was a huge contributor to the organization. She had helped with services for Keono and his recovery as well as fears of suicidal thoughts. His dad and mom lost one military son to suicide and were not going to lose another. They all became so close, and since Kai didn't have family, the Shadens seemed to adopt her as a daughter.

She watched the two men sparring back and forth, and even though Thermo was a lot bigger and taller than Keono, Keono stood his ground. It wasn't until they were both sweaty and Keono was breathing heavy that he called mercy.

"I know you were taking it easy on me, man, but shit, where is all that hostility coming from? I swear, Kai and I are just good friends. She's like family. I only wanted to feel her up and kiss her a few times," he teased.

"What?" Thermo asked, all pissed off.

She was shocked at the obvious jealous expression and reaction, but also felt a little giddy about it. Big bad tough guy had emotions. Interesting.

"Don't listen to a word he says. He's always trying to cause trouble. He never once hit on me, and if he did he knew I would kick his butt." She grabbed her bag.

"True. She would, but what a way to get my ass kicked."

Thermo shook his head.

"Come on, let's hop in the pool and grab some lunch. I'm glad you two know one another. I'd be pissed if you didn't get along," Keono said, and as they headed out of the dojo Thermo once again had that uneasy feeling like he wasn't good enough for Kai at all.

When they got to the pool no one was around. Keono pulled off his shirt and got out of his sweats. He was wearing swim trunks underneath.

"Last one in has to make and serve the drinks," Keono said.

Kai started to pull off her T-shirt and sweats, and holy shit, Thermo stopped undressing and watched as her body came into full view. She wore a black bikini, the top just barely held her full, round breasts that were pushed together in a deep cleavage. She was well endowed and then some, and her body was perfection. Tight abs, all definition obviously from training and working out like she did. She even had definition in her calves and her ass. He took it all in. The belly ring, and a tattoo. Holy shit.

She jumped in and Keono was laughing. "Well, I knew that was going to happen," he said.

Thermo kept the t-shirt on, had his swim trunks underneath and then dove into the pool. The temperature was not cold enough to take away the heat in his body, or the lust he felt.

When Kai emerged from swimming underwater, her gorgeous blue eyes, the color so bright and spectacular, looked stunning. Especially with drips of water on her eyelashes enhancing the glow. Her skin was sun kissed, but not overly tan.

She looked at him and the fact he wore a T-shirt and once again he had his reservations, but then Keono started talking about how he and Kai met, and it only added to the attraction Thermo felt for her.

They sat in the pool a little while just talking and then decided to grab those drinks before lunch. When they got out to dry off, he watched her again, finding it difficult to take his eyes from her, but then he heard the whistle and Keono's brothers Bronco and Rhett arrived. They shook hands hello and then greeted Kai with a kiss and a hug. Again, he was jealous, and watched that their hands didn't come too close to her ass, but they didn't. They hugged her like gentlemen. He didn't feel gentlemanly, he felt barbaric. Like lifting her up, pressing her up against the cabana wall and ravishing her mouth, and then maybe her breasts next. He had to turn away. He walked over to the cabana as the others talked and he changed into a new T-shirt and a pair of cargo shorts. When he walked out, Kai was wearing a cover-up, something shear that was see through but classy, like her.

Bronco was in his police uniform and Rhett was plain clothes but wearing his badge, gun and handcuffs. He worked with a special crimes unit.

"So, you two know one another then? That's crazy," Bronco said and Kai exhaled.

"What? Is it a big deal or something? I mean Keono was all worried that the two of you wouldn't get along and here you two are knowing one another. Makes things easier I think," he said, and popped a carrot into his mouth. Their mom must have brought out some food. Sure enough, Keono's parents came out with stuff to cook on the grill.

"I got that, Dad," Keono said.

"I can help, too. You know I love grilling," Kai said.

"No, no, you and Thermo sit and talk. We'll handle this," Mrs. Shaden said, and Thermo squinted at them and then looked at Keono who chuckled.

"Mom, Dad, Thermo and Kai already know one another," he told them, joining them at the grill.

"What?" Canton asked.

"Afina and her brothers are friends with Thermo and his brothers. We met the other night at Corporal's," she said to them.

"Corporal's? I thought you said you were never going back there because of that guy that night?" Bronco reprimanded her and placed his hands on his hips and looked pissed.

"Her friends were all there, and of course Thermo and his brothers," Keono said.

"You knew about this?" Rhett asked, and Thermo got the feeling that these men cared about her. But how much? He was making himself crazy and reading into everything. She wasn't even his girlfriend and he was possessive, protective, and jealous.

"Could we not discuss this now? It was fine," Kai said.

"What happened the last time she was at Corporal's?" Thermo asked, and she gave Bronco a dirty look.

"Nothing," she replied.

"Nothing my ass. Two drunk assholes tried to touch her while she was in the bar, and then when she declined they waited for her outside," Bronco said.

"It was no big deal." She tried minimizing it and one look around at facial expressions alone and Thermo knew she was downplaying it.

"No big deal? The front window of the place was taken out, they were going to press charges," Rhett added.

"The guys attacked you?" Thermo asked.

"Oh brother." She covered her face and walked away toward the bar and started to pull beers from the refrigerator. She walked back over, passing one to each of the men including Thermo, who squinted at her, then to Mrs. Shaden and she walked back to the refrigerator for a beer of her own. A Heineken.

"One of the reasons why her and I began training together," Keono told him.

"You are so full of it, Keono. I was trained before you. I was just a little rusty, and that was more than a year ago, so don't even think of adding on fluff to the story." She sat on the stool by the outdoor bar, tapped her beer bottle against Mrs. Shaden's who smiled, and then nodded in agreement. Both women looked at all the men a few feet away.

"You had a bruised cheekbone and a bruise along your breast," Rhett stated in a fierce tone, staring at her.

"What? How serious was this?" Thermo asked. She squinted at Rhett and then shook her head at Keono and Bronco.

"Well son, go on and tell Thermo," Mrs. Shaden said.

"Kai took a few hits as these guys, big ones, tried forcing her to their truck. One of the guy's, a big dude, threw her over his shoulder and she somehow slithered over the front of him, tripped him up and was able to run back toward the bar, except the second guy grabbed her and turned her around and decked her," Bronco told him.

Thermo was getting angry and the guys continued to tell the story.

"She gets up and decks the guy in the nose, then does several martial arts moves on him and breaks his arm. His buddy charges at her, like he's going to tackle her and kill her and she gets down low, makes her move and flips the guy right over her and through the front window of the place," Rhett explained.

"Are you kidding me?" Thermo asked.

"No. Those two men tried to press charges against her for assault. Dumb asses," Canton said and chuckled.

"You could have been seriously injured or worse if they got you into that truck. Where the hell was everyone else?" Thermo asked.

"Drunk." They all responded at the same time including Kai, and then they all started laughing.

Thermo was shocked, but seeing her moves in the dojo with Keono he could believe it. Size didn't matter in a fight—technique, capability, and opportunity were key in every hand-to-hand combat.

"I can't believe I never heard this story before," Thermo said to them.

"That was over a year ago. You and I have been hanging out more and more in the last few months. That was also one of the first nights Kai went to Corporal's. Of course, Ghost and Cosmo adore her and felt responsible for not having any kind of security in place out there," Keono explained.

"They got it on video, Thermo, if you ever want to see it. No sound though," Rhett said.

"Rhett!" Kai yelled at him, got up off the stool and gave his arm a shove. He laughed, and raised his arms in the air laughing.

As they all started talking she walked next to Thermo. "They made me sound badass, but in actuality it was a pretty damn scary situation. I thought about the what ifs a lot. In fact, I stayed clear of Corporal's and even going out for a while. I kind of didn't feel safe being alone, and I thought I had gotten over that moving here three years ago," she said to him.

"Either way it was impressive, and I did see you sparring with Keono and he gets fierce."

"Tell me about it, I thought he gave me a concussion a few weeks ago."

"Liar!" Keono yelled out.

She laughed.

"So where did you live before Mercy?"

"New Jersey, where Afina and I went to college together."

"Any family there?"

She got quiet a moment, and he figured all that had been there was the soldier boyfriend who died.

"No family around New Jersey. I have some relatives, an uncle and an aunt, but never met them. Long story. Life was hard for a long time. Still can be." She took a sip then looked at the others who were laughing and getting ready to grill. He reached out and caressed her shoulder.

She looked at him and he held her gaze and gave a wink and she gave him a soft smile.

"Who is grilling?" Canton asked.

"I'll do it," Thermo said, and they all cheered and Thermo walked over to the grill and outdoor kitchen and looked to see what to cook first. He caught sight of Keono saying something to Kai, and she shrugged her shoulders and he gave her a hug. He didn't feel jealous. He got it. This was her family. They took her in because she helped to save Keono's life.

* * * *

"Thermo, you don't need to follow me home," Kai said to Thermo after they headed down the driveway to their vehicles. Thermo was parked behind her jeep.

She stopped by the jeep and tossed her duffle bag into the back seat.

"It's late, and you shouldn't be going into your place alone. Just in case."

"Uhm, you did hear what I did to the two guys at Corporal's? I think I can handle myself."

"I'd feel better knowing you got home safely. Go ahead and I'll follow." She shrugged her shoulders and got into her jeep. As she drove and he followed she wondered more and more about Thermo. He was so quiet most of the time, but today he talked more, and she had a feeling it had to do with his relationship with Keono and Keono's family. They were good people, and she adored them.

When she got to her driveway at the townhouse, she got out and fixed the roof of the jeep with Thermo's help. He came around to her side as she grabbed her bag and then locked up the jeep.

"That was fun today," she said to him.

"Filled with a lot of surprises," he said, and looked her over. He was so big and intimidating looking. That thick beard, long hair pulled back, and those dark mysterious eyes.

"Well, have a good week," she said to him.

"You too, and hopefully we can see you some time next weekend?" he asked.

"I have that dinner event Friday."

"Zayn's working anyway, so maybe Saturday?"

"Thermo, I'm not really ready for this. I need time. It's been…a while," she whispered."

He held her gaze. "Been a long time for me, too. You're not the only one taking a chance here. The best thing to do would be to spend time together. So maybe Saturday?"

She stared at him. She couldn't say no. "Okay, but slow, Thermo."

He nodded and started to walk away. He abruptly turned back. "Wait, I don't have your number."

She walked to her door and unlocked it. "I have the feeling if you call Keono and tell him I said you could get it from him, he'll believe you," she said and he nodded.

"He fucking better not pull some big brother bullshit."

She laughed and waved goodnight, then headed inside closing the door behind her. She leaned against it and listened to the sound of the diesel engine in his truck slowly get quieter until she could no longer hear it.

Her heart was racing, her body tingled, and a stupid giddy feeling filled her insides. She was seriously considering a ménage relationship with three badass, six-feet-four military soldiers, and one was even in law enforcement? Had she lost her mind? She threw her hands up into the air and exhaled. This was going to be the longest week of work ever.

Chapter Six

"I heard from my brother. Kai Devaro went to speak with my nephew Monday morning. She's helped him all week, Chadwick. She even got him in with a specialist and they feel he needs medication to help deal with his anger issues. She got him a new therapist, too. I'm amazed, Chadwick. Thank you so much," John Sander told Chadwick.

"I'm so happy to hear the news. I hope it all works out for your nephew, Kenny. I'll be sure to pass your thank you on to Kai."

"Thanks again, Chadwick."

Chadwick ended the call as he walked into the main area of the hospital. He stopped the moment he saw Kai walking toward the coffee lounge area with her friend Amelia and two other women. He glanced at his watch. He had a little time before his meeting so he headed after them. As they started to go toward the coffee station he got her attention.

"Kai," he called out and she looked up, so did her friends, and he could have sworn one of them, Casey, swooned over him. She started fanning herself and went flush.

"Chadwick, how are you?" Kai asked, and stepped from the line.

"I'll get your coffee for you, Kai. Dr. Hayes, do you need anything?" Amelia asked.

"No thank you, Amelia. I just need Kai a moment," he said, and then kissed her cheek hello and took her hand and walked her over toward the wall and away from everyone.

"You are amazing. I just heard from John Sanders. He told me what you've been up to this week, Kai. You've gone above and beyond what we discussed over the phone Sunday night."

"He's such a great guy, and I had seen some similar things before with other soldiers. It isn't his fault, he just needs a little help to handle the outbursts."

"Well, I hope it helps him. I know your objective with Guardians Hope. So are you ready for tomorrow night?"

"The awards ceremony? I guess so. How about you? You're the one being honored and getting an award."

Chadwick was very attractive, with dark hair and baby blue eyes. His skin was flawless, and she wondered if he used facial creams and things like women did. It was just too perfect.

"I think we should go together. You know, to get through it."

She giggled. "Seriously? You can walk out right after your award if you want and no one would say a word. In fact, you could have someone else show up to receive the award for you and that wouldn't even taint your name."

"I'm not like that though."

"No, you aren't, and if you were, we more than likely wouldn't be friends," she said, and smiled.

He took her hand and pulled her close then whispered into her ear. "I've wanted to be more than friends for quite some time. Accept my offer and be my date tonight. It could be the start of something amazing."

She pulled back. "Chadwick, you know I don't date. I'm not ready to."

"It's been several years since your boyfriend passed, surely you have needs."

"What does that mean? Like you want me as a bedmate, Chadwick?" she snapped at him.

He looked her over. "I can get any woman as a bedmate, Kai. It would be more than that."

"I'm sorry, but your…offer doesn't appeal to me at all. I hoped everything works out with Kenny," she said to him.

He pulled her close when she was about to walk away. "Don't get angry with me. We're friends, and I don't want to ruin that. Just tell me if there's someone else."

"I have met someone, but that's it. Nothing more because I'm not ready for more."

"I'm not a patient man."

"I've noticed that." She looked over her shoulder at her friends who were watching. It annoyed him.

"You're at my table tomorrow night. We'll talk more about this slow thing, okay."

She gave him a nod, and he was disappointed but not giving up. Kai would be perfect on his arm, and as his woman.

* * * *

"What the hell was that all about?" Amelia asked Kai when she joined her friends at the table.

"Sex," she said, and Casey nearly choked on her coffee.

"He came straight out and wants to have sex with you?" Amelia asked.

"Basically. He wants me to be his date for the awards ceremony tomorrow night."

"And you said yes, right?" Casey asked.

"No. I said no. I told him that I wasn't ready to date. He proceeded to tell me I was more than ready, and that it has been several years since my boyfriend died."

"What? That jerk said that to you?" Casey asked.

"He totally wants you in his bed," Amelia stated, looking and sounding annoyed.

"Well, that isn't going to happen. I don't need him, and surely he doesn't need me."

"But he wants you. Maybe it would be a good pre-work out to the real deal with someone you actually have feelings for?" Casey said.

"Casey, seriously? She isn't a whore, and she isn't going to come out of the celibacy stint for just anyone. Even though Dr. Hayes is super fucking gorgeous and holy crap, rich, sexy and he was military. An officer actually," Amelia added.

"Oh brother. You two are nuts," Kai said, and then looked down at her cell phone. She felt her face go flush.

"Who is that, Chadwick texting porn to you?" Casey asked, and they laughed.

"No, it's Zayn. Him and the guys are going to Corporal's tonight for wing night."

"Damn woman, you decide to get back into the dating game and your choices are a doctor or three Special Forces soldiers seeking to share you in a ménage. Holy shit. I wish I was you," Casey said.

Kai shook her head. "I'm not ready for any man. Not one and certainly not three."

"You like them though, but you don't have the same feelings for the lust doctor?" Casey asked.

"The lust doctor?" Amelia asked before Kai could.

"Yeah, you know the rich doctor looking for sex with only hot women."

"So wing night tonight it is. I'll text Lionel to see if he can go, too. He's been acting funny lately," Casey said.

"Probably stress at work," Amelia said, and took a sip from her coffee cup.

"He works at a gym. How the hell stressful can that be?" she asked, and texted him.

"Tell them you're game, and we'll be your bodyguards to keep them at bay," Casey added.

Amelia and Kai laughed, but Kai did want to see them. She actually couldn't wait to see them. That giddy feeling filled her core as she texted Zayn back.

* * * *

A few hours later, Amelia, Casey, and Kai were driving in Kai's jeep when Casey screamed for her to stop the jeep right before the entrance to Corporal's parking lot. At first, Kai didn't know why, but then Amelia gasped as she saw a guy with a young woman pressed up against a sports car, and his hand under her skirt, obviously stimulating her.

"Let me out. Park the jeep and let me out!" Casey yelled.

Kai pulled into the parking lot of Corporal's and Amelia let Casey out, then she followed. Kai locked up the jeep and grabbed her purse, but before she even got close enough, Casey shoved at the guy and then pushed the girl away from him.

"You slut, that's my boyfriend. And you jerk, how long have you been cheating on me?" she demanded to know.

"You work all the time, Casey. I got needs."

"You have needs? We were together last night."

"He was with me this morning, this afternoon, and now," the other woman said in a snarky tone.

Casey shoved her.

"Don't do that, Casey. There's enough of me to go around," he said, and then looked at Amelia and Kai.

Casey punched him and he turned around ready to hit her when Amelia grabbed her, his fist hit her shoulder hard and Casey cried out.

"You need me, Casey. You're nothing without me, bitch!" he yelled at her.

"Take her inside, Amelia," Kai said as Amelia started walking Casey into the place. A few people were walking into the bar and saw what happened.

"Stay clear of her. It's over."

"You don't tell me to stay clear of my woman!" he yelled at Kai.

"It's obvious you don't give a shit about her. So be with this one and leave Casey alone," Kai said, and she could tell he was pissed. He started swearing and then began to pace. Kai went inside.

She headed toward her friends when she spotted Zayn talking to some other guys. She gave a wave but then put her finger up like she needed a minute. When she felt the hand grab her arm and pull her back she saw it was Casey's boyfriend. "We aren't done talking," he yelled at Casey.

Kai jumped in his way. She pressed her hands against Lionel's chest. "Lionel, calm down before you do something stupid."

"He already did something stupid. He cheated on me and he hit me," Casey yelled.

Lionel went to step forward when out of nowhere Thermo grabbed him by his shirt and yanked him back.

"You put your hands on her?" he demanded to know.

"Thermo, it's okay. He's leaving," Kai said to him.

"Let go of me and mind your fucking business. What is this shit?" Lionel demanded to know.

"Please, Thermo, it's okay. He's going to leave," Kai said to him.

He stared at her and she hoped he would put Lionel down. He did and Lionel pointed at Casey. "Right now, bitch. Get your ass over here and let's go!"

"No. You hit me. I want nothing to do with you. Leave or I'll press charges." Casey yelled at him.

By now a crowd formed and this idiot didn't realize he was surrounded by cops and soldiers.

Thermo stepped forward. Kai pressed her hands to his chest. She could see the anger in his eyes and now two other men came over and asked the guy to leave or the police would be called. She stared way up into his eyes.

"It's okay, Thermo. He's going to leave," she said to him, and he settled down as the two guys started walking Lionel out, but then Lionel pulled from them in a rage, and he struck Casey again. Thermo grabbed Lionel and punched him, knocking him onto the ground and he was out cold. She grabbed onto Thermo as did his brothers Zayn and Selasi, and she knew in that moment that Thermo had a temper, and was not a man to reckon with. The place erupted in claps and praise and Zayn and Selasi walked toward Lionel and the men lifting him up while they waited for the police to come.

Kai was shaking and looking at Thermo in shock, yet her body was aroused. He growled, grabbed her hand and started pulling her along with him. She didn't know what he was going to do, and she felt so much. Arousal, intimidation, a twinge of fear, wondering what a soldier like Thermo was capable of. They passed by their friends, and other guys they knew and he brought her down the hallway and to the side, lifted her up, pressed her against the wall and kissed her. Her heart was racing, her body on fire at his shocking reaction, but she kissed him back, ran her fingers through his hair as he rocked his large, thick hips against her body, spreading her thighs. The tightness of her jeans added to the stimulation she felt in her pussy. Her thighs were shaking, his hold so tight, his mouth and tongue demanding as he ravished her. Thermo was huge and she was so small in comparison. He could hold her with one hand on her ass and it turned her on.

She felt feminine, protected, but also vulnerable. He moaned into her mouth, his thick beard tickled her skin, but aroused her at the same time because it felt wild, manly, and dominant. Just as she thought that thought, he cupped her breast with one hand and squeezed her ass cheek with his other hand, and rocked his hips against her. She moaned into his mouth and he plunged his tongue deeper, then slid his palm from her ass up her back to her head and tugged on her hair. She pulled from his lips.

They were both panting for breath.

"Thermo," she whispered in a husky sexy tone she didn't mean to do.

"Fuck," he said, and pressed his mouth to her neck, then back up to her lips again. Then along her neck and into her top, that beard, so rough had a way of stimulating her skin and making it feel more sensitive. She felt his tongue lick between her breast and then nip her skin.

"Thermo. Oh God, we need to slow down."

When they heard deep voices she tightened up, and gripped his shoulders of steel that were so thick and hard she barely covered part of it with her small hand.

"Mine," he whispered with eyes narrowed.

Her heart pounded inside of her chest and despite fearing that someone was coming and would see her pressed up against the wall, she didn't let go of him as he lowered her to her feet. She had tears in her eyes and felt overwhelmed with emotional shock. "I got you. Easy," he said to her, caressing her hip bone under her top with his thumb. The voices sounded like they were coming closer. He helped her fix her top as he kept one forearm above her head, and his huge body encased hers, covering it from view. She looked up at him as she fixed her top and then the guys walked closer, saw Thermo and her there and commented.

"Good shot, Thermo. The guy needed his ass kicked."

Thermo nodded and then his stare alone must have sent the message for them to get lost and they did.

Kai couldn't believe how she felt. She reached up as he stared down at her. She caressed his jaw. "What have we done?" she whispered.

He eased his free hand from her hip and placed his hand over hers that was against his cheek. He closed his eyes and her heart felt like it stopped beating. He was feeling what she was feeling? He was just as affected as she was? What in God's name happened?

"We got things started, Kai, and I want more. I want it all." He pressed his mouth to hers, but instead of attacking her mouth and practically making her come in his arms, he kissed her tenderly, sweetly, and she actually felt her heart react so she pulled her lips from his and hugged him around the waist, tight.

* * * *

"What's going on back here?" Zayn asked.

Thermo stared at him. Kai was pressed against Thermo, her arms wrapped around his waist and she looked so petite and sexy. He knew that Thermo made a move and him and Selasi would, too.

"Did the police come?" Thermo asked.

"You're good man. Casey is pressing charges. We're just glad that asshole didn't try to hit Kai," Zayn said, and reached out to caress Kai's hair.

"I was fine," she whispered, and her voice cracked, indicating she was emotional.

Thermo pulled back. Selasi stared at her.

"I want to know how things got started, but first things first." Zayn stepped closer, cupped her jaw and cheek, tilted it up toward him before he leaned down and kissed her softly. She grabbed onto his hips and he slid his hand under her hair to the base of her neck and plunged his tongue deeper. Zayn lifted her up with one hand on her ass and pressed her up against the wall.

"I'll go talk to the police. You two watch over, Kai," Thermo said, but Zayn was too engulfed in the effects of Kai's kiss.

The feel of her round, sexy ass, the scent of her shampoo and all the emotions, the attraction they had been fighting. He plunged his tongue deeper and she gripped onto him then pulled from his mouth and hugged him around the shoulders.

"Oh God, I can't believe this is happening."

Selasi caressed her hair. Zayn continued to hold her against the wall but leaned back as Selasi had a handful of her hair, their eyes locked and Zayn knew she was the one for him and his brothers.

"My turn," he whispered, and Selasi lowered his mouth slowly to Kai's and kissed her next.

She was light, sexy, and Zayn was able to pass her to Selasi to hold and to feel like he had. He watched the hallway making sure no one interrupted this moment, this huge step for all of them and especially for Kai.

He turned and watched his brother caress her thigh to her ass with one hand. The sight made Zayn's dick harden in his jeans. His brother's hand looked huge against her jean-covered thigh and then over her ass. Selasi turned so he was against the wall and it gave Zayn a perfect view of her ass, the low riding jeans, her tanned skin, that tattoo Thermo mentioned, and her sexy little body. She was feminine, hot, and men wanted what was theirs and they needed to set things in motion and claim her theirs tonight.

"Selasi." Zayn heard her moan and could see her pushing on his shoulders, but her head was tilted back and Selasi's mouth was in her top against her breast. She grabbed onto his head.

"It's too much. Please slow down. Please," she begged.

Selasi reacted. He eased his mouth from her breast and hugged her to him, then locked gazes with Zayn.

His brother never looked so intense and like a man who was not going to let go of what he had in his arms. Kai was coming home with them tonight.

* * * *

"You shouldn't be drinking so much," Kai said to Casey.

"I can't believe what happened here, Kai. I'm so embarrassed," Casey said, and downed another shot.

Kai glanced toward the bar behind her where Selasi, Thermo, and Zayn were standing, waiting for her to get back to them. She was still trying to recover from what happened in the hallway, and now their possessive holds on her in public.

"You look scared, Kai. They're Special Forces soldiers, you know that, right?" Amelia asked.

"I know."

"Thermo has that look in his eyes. It was intense and got worse when he thought you were in danger," Amelia stated.

"It was intense, but he didn't lose control," Kai said.

"Because you put your hands on him and he locked onto you. It was amazing," Casey said, and a tear fell from her eye.

"What?" Kai asked.

"We saw it. What did he do to you back there in the hallway?" Casey asked.

She swallowed hard. "He grabbed me, lifted me up, pressed me against the wall and kissed me like a man on a mission."

"Jesus, that sounds so hot," Amelia whispered.

"Zayn and Selasi, too?" Casey asked.

Kai nodded.

"You let them. You enjoyed it, right?" Casey asked.

Kai nodded.

"Be careful, Kai. You haven't been in the dating scene for years. Things are different. Men demand and they want, they lie, they make promises and you think it's perfect and then the next minute they're done with you. That's with one man. Multiple is that many times worse, and that many times riskier," Casey said, and Amelia caressed Casey's hair.

"I think they really like Kai. It's the way they look at her. The way they noticed her the first time they met. Plus, Kai has that look in her eyes, too," Amelia said, and smiled.

Kai hugged Amelia's arm. "I'm so confused. I'm feeling way too much, and I'm scared. Truly scared because of their professions and the danger Zayn is in with the job he has, as well as the effects of war, of serving that Selasi and Thermo appear to have. Thermo the most."

"Slow things down and take your time. No need to rush into bed with them. You want more than just sex, or you would have accepted the doctor's invitation months ago, never mind today," Amelia told her.

"I don't feel for Chadwick what I instantly feel when I'm around Selasi, Zayn, and Thermo," Kai said.

Casey raised her glass, another shot of tequila.

"You owe me, Warrior Angel. I just helped those three hard ass soldiers make a move, and for you to realize you're hot for them and take a chance on whatever it is they want, even if it's just your body. That's huge," Casey said, and Amelia laughed, so did Kai.

"I'm driving you two home, so don't even think of trying to get another ride," Kai said to them.

"Are you sure you don't want to go home with them?" Amelia asked.

Kai shook her head. "I said I need slow. I need to process what happened tonight. If I continue with them, I'm opening myself up to some sensitive issues and memories I have, and even fears. I need time to think."

"Then go be with them now. I give Casey another hour tops, and then we'll be carrying her out of here," Amelia said.

"No way. I'm good for this bottle," Casey said, and then stared at the half drunk bottle of tequila.

"Looks like I'm sleeping over at Casey's tonight," Amelia said, and Kai chuckled.

Kai walked back over toward Selasi, Thermo, and Zayn. The second she was close enough, Selasi pulled her between his legs as he sat on the barstool. Zayn moved in behind her and put a hand on her shoulder and Thermo who sat right next to Selasi, took her hand and placed it on his lap. Her heart began to race once again, practically pound against her chest as all three huge men touched her at the same time. She had to tilt her head back to look up at Selasi.

"She doing okay?" he asked.

"Amelia and I will take her home and stay with her tonight. She's embarrassed."

"Amelia can take care of her. We want more time alone with you," Selasi said, and caressed her skin under her top against her hips.

"I think we need to slow things down."

"No, you're not going to deny what happened between us," Zayn said, squeezing her shoulder and under her hair before pressing his lips to her head.

She leaned back and glanced over her shoulder at him. "I'm not denying it, Zayn. I need time to think things through."

"To push us away," Thermo snapped at her.

She looked at him and shook her head. "To get over the fears, my concerns."

"We can help you with that. We want you with us. We want to feel more of what we had in the hallway, but in privacy. Come home with us tonight," Selasi said to her.

"No."

"Why not?" Zayn asked.

She turned slightly so she could look at him, as well. She was now standing sideways between Selasi's thighs. She pulled Zayn's hand to her hip. Selasi pressed his palm to her belly, and she put her hand on Thermo's thigh and he covered it with his hand.

She closed her eyes and breathed. "This feels incredible. To have the three of you touch me and for me to feel so much. But…I need to go slow. Every bit I feel I fear."

"Do we scare you?" Thermo asked.

She looked at him. "All three of you do."

"Why? Do you think we're capable of hurting you like Casey's boyfriend?" Selasi asked, and he sounded insulted.

"No. I…oh God how do I admit this to you to make you understand?"

"It's about your ex-boyfriend being a soldier like us?" Zayn asked.

"Yes," she said.

"Baby, you can't deny what we feel because of that," Zayn said to her.

"There are multiple reasons, and I know I'll need to share them with you, but I'm not the type of woman to jump into bed with one man never mind three."

"So it's the ménage thing?" Selasi asked.

"Add it to the list."

"The list?" Thermo asked, and squeezed her hand.

She looked around them but no one seemed to be paying them attention.

"I have a lot of fears and a lot of things to work out. I...I only had one lover ever. I gave my heart and soul to him besides my body. It was sacred, and deep, and the reason why I haven't been with any other man in more than three years."

Thermo squinted at her. Selasi's eyes widened and Zayn caressed her lower back under her top. He leaned down and kissed her shoulder.

"It's going to be torture not taking you home tonight, but I get it. We'll work it out. We'll spend more time together, and you'll see this is real," Zayn said to her.

"I'm not playing games or anything. It's how this has to be," she whispered.

Thermo just stared at her, and she could see the walls go up. She hurt his feelings, but then a few of Devin's friends came over and started talking to them. Not going home with Thermo, Zayn, and Selasi was the smart thing to do. They were complicated men. Hard, and even standing here between them, allowing them to show a bit of possessiveness as the men spoke about the job and the case they completed, she felt scared for them all. She just wasn't sure being involved with men like this was a smart move. After all, she loved a soldier with all her heart, body and soul, and even that wasn't enough to keep him from taking his life. How the hell could she make three soldiers like these happy?

* * * *

"I wish she was here right now," Selasi said to Zayn and Thermo.

"I slept like shit," Zayn said.

"It's me she's afraid of," Thermo added.

"What? Why would you say that?" Zayn asked.

"You didn't see the look in her eyes when I knocked out Lionel. She was shaking."

"She stopped you in your tracks before that and after. She calmed you. You reacted to her voice, to her, not any of us. You've never reacted to any woman like you do with Kai," Selasi told him.

"I don't know if this is going to work out. She has too many fears. Too many reservations and she is already comparing us to her dead boyfriend," Thermo stated.

"That's natural for her to do so. He committed suicide. She loved him. She told us how much and that he was her only lover. That's deep and heavy, and she probably lives with feeling like she couldn't save him. Don't you think that's part of why she has dedicated her life to creating Guardians Hope and First responders?" Zayn said to them.

"She can't save every soldier and cop with PTSD or a fucked up mind because of the shit we all go through." Thermo raised his voice.

"That may be the case, but perhaps it's her way of healing and getting closure. We represent two types of men she lost. Her boyfriend who was a soldier and her brother who was a state trooper."

"Keono told me about her brother and how he was gunned down in the line of duty," Thermo said.

"So us being soldiers aren't her only fear. Me being in law enforcement and aiding in the position I'm in is a fear, too. Don't you remember how she spoke with Devin at the barbecue? She was upset at seeing him hurt. She shied away from us big time," Zayn added.

"We have to help her to see that she doesn't need to be afraid. That we aren't going to get hurt, or lose our minds because of what we saw and experienced in the military, and because of your current position, Zayn," Selasi said to them, then stood up and leaned against the kitchen counter. He crossed his arms in front of his chest.

"I still have nightmares and shit. If we do convince her to trust us and let us into her heart and we're in bed sleeping after making love, what if I snap?" Thermo asked with real concern and emotion is his voice.

"You won't," Selasi stated with confidence.

"We'll be there with you. A ménage works for a lot of men like us that have remaining effects of the military. We'll have one another's backs, and Kai will handle it," Zayn said.

"Like she handled you in Corporal's last night," Selasi teased.

He flipped Selasi the middle finger and they laughed.

"The woman has power," Thermo said.

"The woman is going to be ours. We just need to be patient, and I for one, believe she is worth it," Zayn said.

"Agree," Selasi stated.

"Agree," Thermo said.

Chapter Seven

Chadwick Hayes stopped walking and talking the moment he spotted Kai Devaro. She was being greeted with hugs and kisses hello from both women and men who were part of the board, and others who were involved in law enforcement.

She looked stunning. Absolutely stunning.

He stared at her in awe of her beauty, the long, slim fitting, black evening gown enhanced her incredible body. The deep cleavage of her dress was slightly hidden by a sheer piece of champagne material, but any fool could see she was well endowed. As she turned to greet two men and a woman from behind her, the dress got even more amazing, dipping low against her back, revealing her toned, fit muscles and that incredible ass many men spoke about. The dress was classy, sexy, sophisticated, too sophisticated for the men that were here this evening. Except for him of course.

He made his way to her, grabbing two glasses of champagne from the waiter walking around as he passed him by. She would look perfect by his side. He had to convince her to spend time with him and to realize how great a couple they would make. "Excuse me, Miss Devaro, you look absolutely stunning this evening." He passed her a glass of champagne and leaned forward to kiss her cheek hello.

"As do you, Dr. Chadwick." She smiled softly.

She didn't have a clue what she did to him. How badly he wanted to kiss her, hold her in his arms, take her to bed. He always got what he wanted, and despite him needing to leave in the next week or so for Africa and a humanitarian trip he did every year, he still hoped to get a little taste. She was sweet and she would wait the three weeks for his return, or better, he would send for her to join him and she would see that he was giving and caring to those less fortunate, just like she was.

"Dr. Chadwick, congratulations in advance on the award you're receiving. You have done such amazing work. I heard that you did a spectacular job on a gunshot wound to the chest near the heart, that other doctors wouldn't have touched and gave up on the patient," Ken Willson said to him and in front of Kai. It made her lovely blue eyes widen in shock. He couldn't have paid the man to say something so perfect right now.

"Yes, it was indeed a very risky operation, but considering the man would die, his family chose to take the shot and it was a successful operation. I'm hoping that he'll recover completely, but it's going to be a long recovery process for him."

"Amazing. Excuse me please," Ken said, and walked away leaving him alone with Kai.

He placed his hand on her hip. "You are the most beautiful woman in this place, Kai," he said to her, and she smirked.

"And you are a complete flirt, Dr. Chadwick."

"Are we back to such formalities because I told you how I feel about you?" he asked, and she took a sip of champagne so he took one, too.

"It changes things, Chadwick."

"How so?"

"I think of you as a very good friend. Someone I can talk to and count on for advice with clients, with anything medical, and you want something different now that I can't give you."

He tapped her hip.

"You can give it to me, and I guarantee it will be perfect. Come on, we'll talk more before this thing gets started.

He guided her through the crowds of people, and every man took in the sight of her, smiled and said hello, and the women looked at her with envy.

"Dr. Chadwick, so nice to see you made it this evening, especially with your trip to Africa right around the corner," Mary Phelps said to him, and then she looked at Kai.

"Kai Devaro, meet Mary Phelps, her husband Peter is the top neurosurgeon in the country, and she is a huge contributor to my program I do overseas in third world countries treating those with grave medical needs. You two should talk later. Mary, Kai is the coordinator and founder of Guardians Hope," he said, and Mary smiled wide.

"Oh my goodness, I recently heard a story about John Sander's nephew. That was the first I heard of this organization. I would love to find out more. Could we possibly get together to discuss things, or perhaps Chadwick can bring you along to lunch this week at the country club? I'll have several of my friends there who would all love to assist I am certain."

"That is so kind of you, Mrs. Phelps."

"She'll be there. I'll make sure of it, and hopefully Meredith Walker as well. She would go head over heels for Kai's ideas."

"I bet she would, too. I'll be sure Meredith is in attendance. Enjoy the evening both of you. She's stunning, Chadwick," Mary said, and smiled and then walked away.

"Oh my God, Chadwick, I can't believe that just happened."

He smiled at her as he continued to guide her toward their table. "Believe it. You and I would make a great team. I can help to introduce you to some very influential people willing to put money into your programs because they actually work."

"Chadwick."

He stopped her by the table. "You have amazing ideas, your success rate is commendable, but you can do so much more and that takes money, donations and staff. Many of the people who are part of the country club and meet each week for this luncheon Mary mentioned, are the kind of people with deep pockets but also big hearts. Plan on attending with me and I guarantee you'll be blown away and realize what I say is true. Together we can do so much." He brought her hand to his lips and kissed the top of it.

* * * *

"What the fuck?" Devin yelled out as Zayn spoke to him over the earpiece.

"Hold your position with the others. We got movement in the backyard, across the way, and the other team just picked up on—"

The gunshots ricocheted against the wall right above Devin's head.

"Get down!" he yelled to the others. I front door of the building burst open, the window on the side, just a few feet from where he and two men were. The men inside had guns and they were shooting at the police, at Devin and his team.

"We're coming in hot," Zayn said, and they did just that, counter fired into the building and against the men by the door and window. They took them out and the orders were given to move in to arrest Mark Garci who was wanted for federal and local charges of rape, murder, and drug operations. He was one badass catch if they could capture him. They had been hunting for more than fourteen months when they got this tip. Devin had his weapon drawn and was moving into the house. Shots were fired and him and the team and now Zayn and others were going through each room and catching multiple gang members but no sign of Mark.

Devin cut the corner and his partner Johnny was right behind him. He glanced Zane's way and shots rang out. Zayn shot his weapon and moved toward the danger and out of Devin's line of sight. As Devin and Johnny checked their room, the shot came from the right, hitting his chest and his shoulder and sending him flying back against the wall. He couldn't focus. The pain was so intense. More gunfire then yelling and the next thing he knew he was surrounded by cops and paramedics and he couldn't respond. He closed his eyes.

"Fight, Devin. Fight!" Zayn said to him, and he could see Zayn holding his arm, and there was blood. He looked down but then rolled his head to the right, trying to fight the darkness pulling him forward as pain radiated against his chest. He could hardly catch a breath.

Darkness, then silence.

* * * *

Kai was clapping for Chadwick as he received his award, said a few words, and then returned to the table. She was filled with mixed emotions resisting the pull to be with Selasi, Zayn, and Thermo, and if they were right for her. A ménage was serious. Once she engaged in that there would be no turning back. One man was difficult enough to feel attracted to, and as fearful as she was about their professions and Zayn being in law enforcement, she did find it attractive and honorable. She really needed to spend more time with them before she jumped into bed with them. She looked at Chadwick as he spoke to the other people at their table. All pretty well off, and so different than her and where she came from, and what she struggled to get through. These people really didn't know poor, or struggling to make ends meet or just to eat. She used to be envious of them. Of people like this. It had started out her goal in life to not be lower class or to struggle financially. She budgeted everything out and she wanted for nothing, but a man like Chadwick had it all. He wasn't complicated. She understood him. He was attractive, successful, and he obviously found her attractive.

He represented the things she had hoped for in life, the kind of man she would had picked out that wouldn't make her fearful, or needy. But did she have feelings for Chadwick like she did for Zayn, Selasi, and Thermo?

Her thoughts were interrupted as she saw a couple of law enforcement officers she knew leave their tables. Something was going on. She got nervous instantly, and looked at Chadwick.

Her cell phone rang. "It's Afina." She answered it and got up from the table to walk to the hallway.

"Kai, it's Devin, he was shot and it's bad."

"Oh my God, how? When?" she asked as tears filled her eyes. She looked up and Chadwick was there with her purse in his hand.

"Thirty minutes ago or so. I just got here to General, and there are police everywhere, the media, too. Oh God, Kai, Zayn got shot, too."

"Zayn?" She felt her body shaking.

"I think he isn't as bad as Devin, but we don't know. It's so crazy here, and Mike can't get any information."

"I'm coming now," she said.

"I'll drive your jeep. Where are the keys?"

"Chadwick, Devin was shot and my friend Zayn, too."

"Okay, I'll call on the way. We'll see who is on. It's at General?"

"Yes."

She was shaking so hard. This was what she feared. She even told Devin to be careful. Now he was shot, Zayn, too? What if something happened to them? What if they die? She can't do this. She can't be more than friends with men who engage in this type of profession. She can't lose men she cares about.

"Dr. McAndrews is in the E.R. and he's still evaluating the situation. I can't speak to him so when we get there I'll see. It will be okay."

When they pulled into the parking lot is was covered with police and the media. Chadwick walked her into the main area and Mike, Turner, Fogerty, Selasi, and Thermo were with Afina. She got to her with Chadwick close behind, but then he walked right to the main nurse's station. She hugged Afina tight. "It's bad," Afina said, and started crying.

She pulled back, felt the hand on her waist, and Mike was there.

"We don't know anything, but the doctor on call isn't saying much," Mike said, and hugged her. She pulled back. "Zayn is going to be okay. Just a flesh wound to his upper arm."

She turned to see Selasi. "I can't believe this."

He pulled her into his arms and hugged her tight. "It will be okay. Zayn just needs some stitches. We're glad you're here."

She was filled with mixed emotions, but then a doctor came out of the main doors and Mike went over to him. Afina grabbed Kai's hand and they went along with Thermo, Selasi, and the others.

"Investigator Stelling is in critical condition. Despite the bulletproof vest he was wearing, the one bullet to the top left went through and damaged arteries to his heart. At this time, we're trying to decide what will be best for him, but it's not looking good."

Afina started to cry harder and Kai held her tight until Mike pulled her into his arms. Selasi hugged Kai from behind and then her eyes landed on Chadwick who squinted. She pulled from Selasi's arms and walked to Chadwick.

"Chadwick, it's my best friend's cousin. Can he be saved? Is there anything you can do?" she asked him.

He stared at her and then over her shoulder and she knew he was looking at Selasi and Thermo. He would figure out that they cared about her. Chadwick cupped her cheek. "I'll talk to McAndrews and find out everything. I'll see what I can do."

She hugged him and she felt his hand slide over her ass as he released her, and he walked through the emergency room doors like he owned the place.

"Kai, what did Dr. Hays say?" Afina asked her as she continued to cry. "Can he save him? Can he do something?"

"He said he's going to find out. If he can he will."

"He will. For you, he will," Afina said.

* * * *

"So who the fuck is that doctor?" Selasi asked Mike.

"He's one of the top emergency surgeons in the country," Turner told them.

"Kai knows him well?" Thermo asked.

"They're friends, have been for years, but I'm not going to lie, Afina mentioned several times the guy wants her in his bed," Mike said.

"Fuck," Selasi stated and ran his fingers through his hair.

"You're making progress with her though," Mike added.

"She'll freak out because of this. Close up again, and put up the walls, because this is one of her fears and why she doesn't want to get involved with us," Selasi told them.

"She'll get over that. You three and Kai are perfect for one another, and the attraction can be seen and felt within seconds of watching you. Make her understand and realize that things happen, but Zayn is okay and you guys aren't doing anything risky," Turner said to them.

Just then Zayn walked out of the main doors of the E.R. with his shoulder and arm bandaged up and a handful of papers and a white bag. They greeted him with hugs and slaps on the back, after other officers greeted him first. Afina walked over as Kai stood with her arms crossed and red-rimmed eyes, just staring at him. Afina hugged him and then Zayn told her he was okay.

"Devin is in bad shape, Zayn," Afina said to him.

"He'll pull through. I heard some big shot surgeon is scrubbing up and getting ready to operate. That he's the best, and someone he cares about is friends with Devin so he stepped in."

"That's what they told you back there?" Thermo asked.

"Said that Devin wasn't going to make it because the surgery would be too risky, but this surgeon checked things out and said the risk was high, but that he was going to give Devin a chance to live through this, and the only choice was surgery or giving up. Sounds like an amazing doctor that just happen to be in the ER tonight," Zayn said.

"Not just happen to be here. Kai brought him here. She was at the awards ceremony and he drove her here when he heard what was going on," Afina said to him.

He looked at Kai and went toward her, and Selasi saw she took a step back.

"Kai?" Zayn questioned, and she reached out and went to touch his bandaged arm as tears fell. Zayn pulled her into his arms and hugged her tight.

"It will be okay," Mike whispered to Selasi.

Selasi looked at Thermo, and no words were exchanged. They had a bad feeling the walls were already up once again.

* * * *

Hours passed, and Kai leaned against Amelia who showed up with a change of clothes for Kai, but she hadn't gotten undressed yet. She could hear the men talking, and the officers coming and going from different shifts or stopping by with coffee and food, all the things first responder families do when one of their own is in need. As she watched them and listened, she saw the camaraderie, the family bond they all shared and she respected that. Her heart was aching every time she looked at Zayn, Selasi, and Thermo. She longed to be held in their arms, yet she resisted out of fear of this situation. What if it were Zayn in there too right now? Touch and go? Near death? Then what? She just didn't think she could take this emotional roller coaster and the fears that came along with being the woman to a cop, a soldier, and man in a dangerous profession, never mind multiple.

She thought about Chadwick and the things he said to her. The people he knew and the things that were safe and normal to engage in and be a part of. Did she really need all this drama and fear and worry all the time? She would be a nervous wreck every time Zayn left for work from now on whether she was his woman or not. Chadwick was a safer choice. But her feelings for him were nothing in comparison to Zayn, Thermo, and Selasi.

The doors to the E.R. opened and there stood Dr. McAndrews and Chadwick, as well as two other men. They were perspiring, but Chadwick looked cool as a cucumber, confident and serious. She stood up with Amelia and Afina and the men and they walked over to them.

"Surgery was a success, thanks to Dr. Hayes," Dr. McAndrews stated, and Kai covered her mouth with her hand as tears fell. He went on to explain what they did, and how delicate and meticulous of a surgery it was, but that Devin was in good shape and the next forty-eight hours would give them more information.

"Thank you so much, Doctors. Thank you," Mike said and shook each of their hands, and the other men followed.

Selasi hugged Kai from behind and she turned in his arms and hugged him back.

"Kai?" She heard Chadwick's voice and turned to look at him, but Selasi kept his arm around her waist. She locked gazes with Chadwick.

"Thank you for all you did to save our cousin," Zayn said to him and then he, Selasi, and Thermo shook Chadwick's hand.

"Kai, come here a minute," Chadwick said to her, and she eased from Selasi's hold. She didn't need to turn around to know they were jealous and pissed, but Devin was safe and he would make it.

Chadwick took her hand and brought it to his lips. "You doing okay?" he asked, and reached up to caress her tears away.

"I'll be okay. I don't know what to say or how to thank you."

He smiled, but glanced at the men feet behind her. "I could think of a few things, but that wouldn't be very professional, or what a friend would do or request." She squinted at him. "I'm getting the eyes of death right now from those men behind you and the one with the beard and tattoos looks like he wants to hurt me."

She chuckled. "They're good friends."

"I think you need to have the same talk you had with me, with them."

"I told you I wasn't ready. That I have a lot of fears."

"I get it now, and I'm sure tonight's incident makes you think I'm a safer choice than him?"

"Then them."

"Them?" he asked.

She shook her head. "Complicated, Chadwick, and a week new."

"Then make no decisions right now. It's been an emotional night, the next few days will lessen as your friend recovers. You plan on that lunch with me this week though. It would be crazy to cancel."

"Okay. I owe you."

"We'll discuss it." She hugged him and he squeezed her tight, and when he pulled back he kept his hand on her hip and then cupped her cheek.

"Need a ride?"

"I'm staying."

"In this sexy dress with all these guys staring at you?"

"I got bodyguards and Amelia brought clothes," she said.

"Okay, we'll talk more tomorrow."

"Sorry you didn't get to enjoy the awards ceremony."

"They'll be others. Besides, the best part was having you with me. I'll call you tomorrow." He walked away so they all could hear.

When she turned around of course all the guys were looking at her not just Zayn, Selasi, and Thermo, but Turner, Mike, and Fogerty. She walked over toward Afina and Amelia. "Everything will work out fine. Chadwick is the best at this. Thank God he was in town."

"Thank God you're such good friends with him," Amelia said, and Kai grabbed the bag to go change in the ladies room.

Chapter Eight

Kai heard the knock on her office door and looked up to see Casey there.

"Hey, Casey. How is it going today?" she asked, knowing how difficult it was for her to come back to work after the incident at Corporal's.

"Hanging in there. It's interesting to be the office gossip instead of the office gossiper," she said, and then walked into the office.

Kai was fixing up her desk and preparing to leave for the luncheon with Chadwick. Then she was going to head to the hospital to get an update on Devin and see Afina, Mike, and the guys, even though Chadwick was keeping her posted.

"You still meeting Chadwick at the country club?" Casey asked.

"Yup, that's where I'm heading now and then to the hospital."

"I know I kind of pushed about sleeping with Chadwick and all, but I think you're making a mistake."

Kai looked toward the doorway. "First of all, I'm not sleeping with Chadwick."

"Not yet, but he's spinning his charm, you're running from your true feelings for Zayn, Selasi, and Thermo, just because you're afraid to get hurt."

"You don't understand."

"I don't understand what? What it is to get hurt? To have my heart broken? To get punched and treated like a whore by the man I thought loved me but was fucking other women? What?" She raised her voice. Then she closed her eyes and breathed.

Kai came around her desk. "I'm not saying anything like that."

"Then why? Why are you pushing away the three men that make you smile, make your eyes shine, and make you look even more beautiful and glowing than I've ever seen you since knowing you?"

Kai covered her mouth with her hand and then leaned against her desk. She stared at Casey. "I don't think I can handle being the woman of a soldier or a cop, and three of them, scares the hell out of me. I can't go through that kind of loss again."

"You mean because your boyfriend who died was a soldier?"

"I can't talk about this. I made a decision and I'm not getting involved with anyone. Not Chadwick and not Zayn, Selasi, and Thermo, either. I'm going to do what I have from the start. Focus on getting services to those soldiers and law enforcement in need, and any first responders who need our help, as well. This luncheon could mean some new funding for future programs and for adding services, buildings and employees to the retreat we have been working on. That's my focus."

"And with all that love and big heart of yours worrying about everyone else, even strangers, what about you? When do you get to be happy, to be cared for, protected and loved, huh? When?"

"I loved once and was loved in return. Perhaps that was all that's meant to be for me." Kai grabbed her purse and then gave Casey a smile. "I'm glad you're back. Let me know if you need anything, and if Lionel starts trying to contact you." Casey nodded and Kai walked out of the office and headed to meet Chadwick.

* * * *

"Where is Kai? Did she come today?" Selasi asked Mike.

"She'll be by later. She had work and a luncheon or something," Mike said and turned away.

"What?" Selasi asked him.

"I think maybe you guys should just give her time and space. This incident freaked her out," Mike said.

"What are you telling me, to give up on her? Not with the feelings we have, and not the feelings she has for us," Selasi said.

"She went to the luncheon with Chadwick," Mike replied, and Selasi was instantly pissed off and jealous. One look at his brothers and they didn't say a word.

* * * *

Kai was trying to be upbeat but her conversation with Casey weighed heavy on her heart. She couldn't worry about herself right now. Not with this luncheon and meeting these wealthy people who were here to learn more about Guardians Hope. She had to focus on the charity and the good it provided for so many. So she spoke and talked to everyone who asked her questions, and the biggest surprise was the checks they wrote on the spot and handed her. Money she hadn't expected, and that brought tears to her eyes.

As she thought about the success and all this could do for the clients, she thought of Zayn, Thermo, and Selasi.

"You have such a huge heart. My God, I loved hearing all about the work you do at Guardians Angels. I want to do more than just give a donation. Can we talk about it more maybe next week?" Mary Phelps said to her.

"I would love that. We can always use volunteers, and with the connections you and your friends have to those in the medical and legal fields, I'm certain we could use whatever they are willing to give, whether that is time, professional advice or whatever."

"Wonderful. I got your number from Chadwick. I'll call you and set things up."

Kai was walking out with Chadwick when he stopped her by the car. He pulled her into his arms and pressed her against the car. She gasped.

"My God you're incredible. They all loved you," he said, and then kissed her. She didn't feel a thing as she pushed on his shoulders and he must have realized it and slowly pulled back.

"Chadwick, I said friends, and nothing more."

"It's those soldiers and the cop right? The three at the hospital that wanted to kill me. You're in love with them?"

"No, I'm not in love with anyone. I don't want this." She stepped from his hold and he pulled her back and she didn't know what he would do.

"God damn it to hell!" He raised his voice and held her by her arms, then lowered his head and exhaled. "You need to make a decision. It's either me, or them. I'm leaving next week for Africa. I can send for you in a week and we can start this off right."

She shook her head. "I don't have those kinds of feelings for you, Chadwick. I'm sorry."

"But you have them for three men? For them?"

"I choose to be alone. That's it."

He stared at her. "I care so much about you. I want what is best for you. Maybe the feelings aren't quite there yet but they could be. We're perfect in all other categories."

She ran her hand up his chest to his shoulder and squeezed it. "All other categories? Listen to yourself, Chadwick. You want a model, a prize, something that looks good on your sleeve. That isn't love. That surely isn't what I want even though it would be easy to fall into a routine, but that isn't fair to me or to you."

He stared down at her and then gave a nod. He pulled back. "Friends still?"

"As long as you don't try to kiss me like that again."

He eyed her over in the beige skirt and camisole she wore with high heeled wedge sandals.

"That might be difficult." He winked and she smiled.

"I'll see you when I get back?"

"You better email me some pictures," she said, and then she got into her car and exhaled. With a heavy heart, she went right to the hospital.

Two hours later, Devin still in ICU and not waking up yet, and with everyone giving her a cold shoulder, she headed home.

She just walked into her townhouse when there was a knock at the door. She peeked through the peephole and was shocked to see Thermo there. She unlocked it and stared way up at him. "Thermo, what are you doing here?"

"We came to see you," Zayn said with Selasi, and they walked into her townhouse. She stepped back and Thermo crowded her. When he reached out to grab her by her blouse she gasped, and then his mouth was over hers, his one hand slid up under her hair and the other around her waist to her ass. He plunged his tongue in deeply, then squeezed her ass and rocked his hips against hers. She kissed him back, filled with fire, with desire and need. It was insanity what these men did to her. He lifted her up and placed her right onto the kitchen table. A chair fell over and then she felt his hand slide up under her skirt against her thigh. He squeezed her hip bone and then pulled from her mouth. She gasped for breath as Selasi cupped her cheek and kissed her next as he leaned over the table.

She felt fingers against her clit and moaned and lifted her pelvis as Thermo ripped her thongs and then slid fingers into her cunt. She cried out her release as Selasi released her lips and then Zayn gripped her jaw and cheek.

"Does he make you come like this? Does he drive you this fucking wild with desire and need? Does he?" he demanded to know, and she knew he was talking about Chadwick.

Tears filled her eyes and she shook her head. "No."

"Fucking right, because you belong with us and we belong with you," Thermo said to her, and then lowered down, spread her thighs, and began to feast on her cunt. She reached for his head, tilted her head back and moaned and shook.

"Ours. You're going to be all ours. No more fighting us, baby. We want and need you. Let go and let us love you," Selasi said to her. The tears fell and another orgasm was building up inside of her.

"Let me taste our woman," Selasi said, and Thermo lifted up and moved only for Selasi to take his place. Selasi's large palms slid up her thighs and he stared at her. "Tell us you're ready to let go. Tell us you trust us and we can work these fears out."

"I'm so scared." She looked at Zayn's arm and the bandage there.

"She needs more convincing," Selasi said, and then lowered down and began to thrust fingers into her cunt and then alternate tongue and fingers. She was rocking her hips as another orgasm hit her. Zayn cupped her cheek as Thermo unbuttoned her blouse and pushed it aside.

"This isn't the first time I've been shot, baby. I love what I do, and shit happens sometimes, but if you ask me to quit the job I'll do it. I'll do it for you," he said, and she cried and then reached up and pulled him down to kiss her.

* * * *

Selasi wanted to cheer. His instincts had been right and he forced his brothers to come here and confront Kai and make her see how much they cared about her.

He eased his mouth from her pussy and then him and Zayn lifted her up. She stood on shaking legs and they undressed her and she helped.

When she was naked in front of them, he licked his lips. "You think my brothers and I were overprotective of you before? Just you fucking wait. You're incredible. Fucking incredible," he told her.

"And ours, momentarily," Zayn said, and cupped her cheeks and kissed her.

Selasi looked at her gorgeous body. The curves, the full breasts, her tight abs and belly ring and that sexy, feminine tattoo of sunflowers and an American flag along her hip. He lowered down and caressed her thighs up and down, then he leaned forward and kissed her pussy, then up to her belly ring. Thermo grabbed her hand and pulled it behind her back, giving him better access to her breast and he began to feast. They were all touching her and getting her used to their touches.

Zayn released her lips. "To the bedroom, where we can spread her out and enjoy every inch of our woman," Zayn said.

Thermo released her breast but not before nipping her nipple and making her gasp. Zayn gripped her around the hips and hoisted her up over his shoulder. He turned with his hand on her ass, giving it a slap.

"Zayn! You're arm."

"I feel nothing, baby, but happiness and pleasure," he said and they all walked into her bedroom.

* * * *

Kai absorbed the scent of Zayn's cologne as he lay her on the bed and hovered over her. His one foot on the floor at the edge and his thigh and knee between her thighs, he slid her arms above her head. That crewcut hair, the fierce expression in his eyes, that well-trimmed beard and all those muscles.

"You're beautiful," she whispered to him.

"You're incredible in every way. Every inch of you." His eyes swept over her body from lips to breasts to her weeping cunt. His brothers were right there, too. Selasi pulled his shirt up and over his head, revealing muscles upon muscles, and he winked at her with those sexy blue eyes, that clean-shaven face with firm lips, distinguished nose, and a total military hottie expression. He was experienced. They all were.

Zayn slid her one arm up above her head. "Stay like that. Obey my orders," he whispered, and for some reason she got wetter, and wiggled her hips and tilted her pelvis up. He chuckled low, knowingly. He caused the reaction and then licked her nipple on that same side. She went to lower her arm only for a fully naked Selasi to lay on the bed beside her and clasp her hand with his and bend it above her head. She turned to look at him.

"You're more than perfect. Look at you, baby. So sexy and in great shape. I love these taut muscles." Zayn released her breast as Selasi eased his palm down over her breast to her abs and then right to her cunt. Zayn spread his thighs, widening her thighs as he lifted his shirt up over his head and tossed it. He undid his pants and she moaned as Selasi slid a finger into her cunt.

He leaned closer.

"You're so fucking wet. Your body knows," he said, and gently pressed his lips to hers.

The bed dipped. She felt Zayn get up and she couldn't look as Selasi was kissing her and fingering her cunt.

She pulled her thighs together and then felt the large, warm hand against her knee.

"Open for us. Show us you're ready," Thermo said, and she did as Selasi released her lips, gave her a wink, and then slid down using his mouth as a pathway over every inch of her left side.

She looked at Thermo as she panted, lips parted and about to come once again.

He was naked from the waist down and stroking his cock, but he wore a shirt and she stared up at him.

"You ready for us? Ready to accept us?" he asked.

She stared at him. "Why the shirt?" she asked, and he squinted.

Zayn eased back up and Thermo reached over and cupped her cheek.

"I have scars, baby. I don't want to ruin this for all of us," he said to her, and then lowered down to kiss her lips. She kissed him back and he lowered between her legs, his cock at her entrance. He pulled up.

"Do we need condoms?" Selasi asked her.

"No."

"You want us to claim you our woman? You accept us?" Selasi asked.

"Say yes," Thermo whispered to her.

"Yes," she said, and she felt him ease his cock into her cunt.

She was shaking, it had been so long and the moment he thrust all the way in, she moaned, locked her legs against his hips, and tears spilled from her eyes.

Thermo was gentle and loving. He took his time and she could feel how hard he was. She was glad she waited to have sex again. Glad to know that it was worth it and that she found these men or rather, they found her. She ran her fingers through his long, reddish-brown hair, his beard tickling her neck, but his cock, so super big, moved in and out of her very wet cunt.

"Faster, Thermo, I can take it. It's been so long."

"I don't want to hurt you," he said, and lifted up and she ran her hands under his shirt and over his back. She felt the deep gashes and her eyes widened.

He shook his head. "Don't."

"It doesn't matter to me. I want you scars and all, just as you want me fears, scars, and all."

He pressed his mouth to hers and rolled to the right so he was underneath her. She lifted up, he held her hands to his chest and he took in the sight of her breasts. She loved the way he looked at her with hunger and need.

"So giving and sexy. Tonight we take you together. It's all in, baby," Selasi said, and started to kiss her neck and then slid his hands up and down her back. When his hands cupped her ass cheeks as she thrust her pussy over Thermo's cock, she came some more.

"Hot damn I love these breasts," Zayn said, cupping on and then lowering down to take a taste. She leaned back and then reached for his cock and stroked it. Zayn widened his eyes and reached for her hair.

"You want to taste me?"

"Yes," she said, and continued to rock her hips.

"I'll do a little exploring," Selasi said, and she felt something cool over her anus. As she lowered her mouth to Zayn's cock as Thermo thrust up into her cunt while holding her hips, Selasi slid a finger into her ass.

"God damn she's incredible," he whispered, and she came just like that and Thermo followed.

She was shocked that Selasi was fingering her ass and that she wanted them to explore her everywhere. To own her in every way. It was erotic and sinful. "I'm there, honey. Pull out if you don't want to swallow," Zayn said, but she gripped his thigh and sucked on him then swallowed as he came.

A moment later as she eased her mouth from Zayn's cock, she felt Selasi pull his fingers from her asshole and then lift her up with one arm, place her on all fours on the bed, and then wedge up behind her. He grabbed a fistful of her hair and suckled against her neck.

"You're in for it. We take you one at a time and then we take you together."

"Yes," she whispered, and heard Thermo and Zayn mumble something, but then Selasi eased his cock into her pussy from behind and then thrust right into her.

She lowered her head, gripped the comforter and relaxed her body as Selasi thrust into her over and over again.

Her breasts bobbed and swayed, her pussy clenched against his cock making him moan.

"So fucking tight and wet. My God, baby, I won't last this first time. I won't," he said, and then stroked a little faster.

"You're so big, Selasi. I can't take it. I can't. Oh!" She cried out her release and he grunted and followed. He hugged her from behind and kissed her shoulder.

He eased out and there was Zayn pulling her into his arms and then underneath him. We're going to be at this all night," he said, and raised her arms above her head and tapped them. She understood it meant to keep them there and she did as she moved her chin to her chest and watched him slowly, teasingly explore every inch of her as he gripped his cock and prepared to make love to her.

* * * *

Zayn swallowed down the intensity of the emotions he felt. He hadn't even made love to her yet, but her mouth was incredible and she seemed so giving. He wouldn't have expected anything less from her than all of her. She was gorgeous from head to toe. From the thick, long locks of reddish-brown hair in abundant curls, to her luscious breasts, full, round and more than a handful, and that well trimmed, wet pussy calling to him right now. He wiggled his tongue over her nipple and then around the areola as she watched him with hooded eyes. Thermo raised her arm up above her head and was kissing her arm and down to her underarm to her breast. Selasi was doing the same thing on her other side and she was definitely finding it difficult to lay still.

"Easy, baby. There's so many inches to explore here," he said, and then slid a finger up into her cunt. She tried closing her legs but he was between them.

"No, no, no, you be a good girl and keep those thighs wide and that pussy wet for us," he said to her.

"Oh please, Zayn. Please make love to me."

"Oh, I love hearing you ask for my cock. I'm going to give it to you really soon. I just want to do a little more exploring," he whispered, and then lifted her one thigh higher up against his hip, and then slid a wet finger from her cunt to her anus. He spread her wider and she gasped and tilted her pelvis upward.

"Such a sexy, tight ass. I'm so glad we brought the lube with us tonight. We're going to get you nice and ready."

"Holy fuck," Selasi said.

He eased his finger in and out of her ass and Kai moaned and thrust her hips.

"You want us together? You sure you're ready for that?" he asked.

"I don't care if I'm ready or not, it feels wild and so good. I want to make you happy."

"Every fucking moment you're with us makes us happy, sweetie." Thermo kissed her lips.

"Let's do this," Zayn said, and then pulled his finger from her ass and thrust his cock into her pussy in one smooth stroke. She moaned aloud and he thrust again and again.

"Get ready. The three of us," he said, and then Thermo ran to the bathroom as Selasi climbed up on the bed.

He watched her breasts bounce and she kept her arms above her head without being ordered to keep them there. As Zayn thrust into her cunt, he ran his palm up and down her cleavage and squeezed her breasts. "Look at you, woman. You're so fucking hot and sexy. I'm going to come fast, especially in that tight ass. Fuck, we need to move." He pulled out and then lifted her up and covered her mouth, kissing her. He slid his hand to her ass and fingered her as she rocked her hips and Selasi got on the bed, legs over the edge and Thermo returned wiping his cock after cleaning up.

He turned her around after pulling fingers from her cunt.

"You ride Selasi good and hard while I get this ass ready. Then you take Thermo's cock into your mouth, you hear?" Zayn demanded.

"Yes. Oh God I can't believe this. Yes!" she exclaimed, and he turned her around and she lowered down to kiss Selasi, who wrapped her up tight and slapped her ass. She widened her thighs and he stroked a finger into her cunt and she rode the digit while Zayn grabbed the lube.

"Got it," he said, and then Selasi eased his finger out and adjusted her hips and lifted her up. She gasped and grabbed onto his shoulder so she wouldn't fall forward and stared down at Selasi.

"Ride his cock, baby. Now," Zayn ordered, and she slid her pussy over Selasi's cock and began to thrust up and down, back and forth. Until Thermo caressed her back and her ass and watched Zayn squeezed some lube onto his finger and then slide it gently into her asshole.

"Oh." She moaned and then slid back over his finger. Zayn gripped her hip on the left and ignored her with his right hand.

"That's it, sugar. Back and forth, up and down. Get a feel for it, then the real thing is coming in," Zayn said, and she moaned louder and louder.

"I'm gonna shoot my load," Thermo stated.

"Not yet. Not until we take her together and it's official," Zayn said, and then Thermo gripped her hair and brought his cock toward her.

"I need, baby."

She nodded and then lowered her mouth to his cock and started to work it into her mouth. Zayn thrust his fingers faster and scissored them to be sure she was okay. She was moaning and so were his brothers and he knew she was ready like they were. He eased his fingers out, and replaced them with his cock and that was it. As he nudged his cock into her asshole, pushed through the tight muscles, she moaned and he slid all the way in.

"Fuck yeah!" Selasi said, and began to thrust upward faster. He had to move or he was coming and he didn't want to disappoint her. He wanted to mark her, claim her and make her never ever want to leave him or his brothers ever. Zayn thrust into her ass as he held her hips in place. Thermo thrust into her mouth and she bobbed her head up and down in sync to Zane and Selasi's thrusts into her body. The moaning, thrusting, and the sound of the bed squeaking all added to the moment and then he was on fire.

"I'm there," Thermo said and came in her mouth. He fell back to the bed moaning and she started panting.

"Oh, oh, oh!" She moaned really loudly.

"Yes," Selasi said and came.

Zane gripped her hips, the ache in his arm getting worse but he wasn't going to miss making love to her and being with Kai. He thrust a few more times and the sight of his dick disappearing into her firm, round ass sent him over the edge and he came grunting and shaking behind her before he lowered over her kissing Kai's neck, and then her back as he eased softly from her ass. Selasi rolled her to her side, sliding his cock from her cunt as Thermo caressed her hip and they held her between them.

"Rest, Kai, it's going to take several times to ease our jealousy and to know you're truly ours. Several," Zayn said, and she closed her eyes and cuddled between them.

Chapter Nine

Kai blinked her eyes open to see Thermo laying there next to her with his eyes closed and his arms under his head. Behind her, Selasi stroked her hip and thigh. She glanced down to see Zayn watching her, his bandaged arm still upsetting to look at. She nibbled her bottom lip then looked at Thermo. She did it. She had sex again, well, it was more than that, and felt deeper. She eased up and felt a little ache. She inhaled. Zayn sat up and so did Selasi. "Kai, are you in pain?" Selasi asked.

"I'm okay." Thermo opened his eyes. "What's wrong?"

"She's in pain," Zayn said.

"No, I'm okay. Just leave it alone," she said to him.

Selasi slid his palm over her waist and pulled her back against his chest. He then slid slightly over her. "Don't you lie to us," he said in that commanding tone of his. That clean-shaven face now had hints of a shadow, making him appear rugged and a little wild, but those blue eyes did her in.

"I don't lie."

He raised an eyebrow up at her and Thermo exhaled then turned onto his side to face her. She looked at him. "What?"

"You lied about how you really felt about us," he told her.

"I didn't lie, I just didn't admit what I felt. There's a difference."

He reached over and gripped her chin. "Are you sore from last night?"

She stared at him. At the tattoos all over his arms, the fact he still wore the shirt, that rugged thick reddish-brown beard and those damn killer eyes. She gulped as he squinted coming across even more serious. "A little."

"Fuck, we shouldn't have taken her together and so many times last night," Zayn stated aloud, and got up in all his naked glory. He was a god. The three of them were gods.

"Get a hot bath ready for her," Selasi said, and then kissed her chin, then down to her breast and belly, and she hoped he was going lower but then he eased up from over her, using all those sexy arm muscles to get up, his thick erection plain as day.

He stepped into jeans and she heard her bath running.

"Bubbles?" Zayn called from the bathroom.

"You have any Epson salt?" Selasi asked.

"In the closet.

"Epson salt's in the closet. Just add a little," Selasi said, and then headed that way.

She watched him and then turned toward Thermo. "So you guys are pro at this?" she asked and didn't know why. One look from Thermo and he somehow looked angrier.

"Don't even try that crap," he snapped at her, and then lifted up and pulled her closer. "Never, and I swear I mean never, have we shared the same woman. You're the first, and the last," he said, and then pressed his lips to hers. She ran her fingers through his hair and he deepened the kiss. As she eased her palms up under his shirt, he pulled back and grabbed them. He leaned back and she lifted up, cringing slightly. "I want to see."

"No."

"Bath is ready," Selasi said, and she looked up past Thermo and knew that he heard Thermo tell her no. She needed to respect Thermo's wishes. She leaned down and kissed his shirt covered chest, and when she went to move she closed her eyes.

"Son of a bitch. You are in pain."

Thermo got up and then lifted her up in his arms. "Thermo, it will be fine. I haven't had sex in three years, and then three men, your sizes, and that many times. Of course I was bound to be sore." She tilted her head up to kiss his chin, but kissed his beard and he stared down at her.

"There's a lot to learn and for all of us to get used to. Your sexy body and our need to claim every inch of you and mark you our woman, and you needing to be honest and tell us if we're being too rough or too demanding in bed."

She narrowed her eyes at him. "Sorry I'm not as experienced as you guys."

"We're not. Our experience and the fact we're a lot older than you will bring you much pleasure, sexy," Selasi said, and gave her ass a slap.

"Selasi!" she scolded.

"Ease on in there, sugar. Then we'll discuss food," Zayn said, and Thermo helped her ease into the tub. She closed her eyes and stepped in, knowing their eyes were on her body and she loved that they complimented her. She eased down and then moaned.

"For crying out loud, there isn't anything this woman does that doesn't make me want to fill her up with cock," Selasi said.

She gasped.

"We feel the same way, let her soak then we'll shower and eat, then back to bed," Zayn said to them.

Thermo reached over and stroked her cheek with his finger. "You take your time and make sure there's no more pain. Next round is slow and easy." He leaned down and kissed her softly on the lips. She watched him walk away, that muscular ass, long, thick thighs and the fact he had to duck to walk in and out of her bathroom did something to her.

"Soak," Selasi said, and then headed out. Zayn remained right there. She glanced at him when he stared at her. She leaned her head back.

"How bad are his scars?" she whispered.

He squinted, and then looked uncomfortable about her question. "When he's ready. Don't push him."

She swallowed hard. His tone, the words he chose, made her think that Thermo has some issues with maybe anger, perhaps PTSD. She got a shaky feeling in her gut. What was she thinking sleeping with three men she really didn't know? She gasped when she felt Zayn's knuckles caress her skin. He narrowed his eyes at her as she looked up toward him. She could tell he was upset at her response.

"How is your arm feeling?" she asked, trying to change the subject, but she didn't think that through. He didn't move his hand. He stroked her cheek again.

"I was fine, Kai. It was a tricky situation but my military experience prepared me."

"This time," she said, and then finished soaping up.

"I know you have fears about my current job. You'll need to understand that this type of work can be dangerous, but more times than not it runs smoothly and everyone's training is perfect. I've personally trained these men."

"You need to know that I do understand this profession. Just like I understand what it is to be a soldier. All it takes is one bullet, one centimeter, one wrong step, one unfathomable experience and you're changed forever or dead. So don't preach to me." She stood and reached for the towel, but when she went to step out he grabbed her and lifted her up into his arms. "Zayn."

"Don't put up the walls. Don't start a fight with me because of your fears and insecurities."

"I'm not." He raised both eyebrows up at her as he set her feet down and helped her to dry off.

She grabbed onto his shirt. He towered over her, big time like this and even with him barefoot and only wearing jeans.

"I lost my brother to some psycho anti cop jerk off who simply chose to attack and shoot him just because he wore a trooper uniform and was in the wrong place at the right time. So forgive me when my response to your whole training thing and being prepared more often than not speech gets a negative response. You can't always be prepared, and I get that. I get the calling, the need to serve, but on the other end of all those guts, the glory, the pride, are people sitting at home, getting ready to celebrate another day, and another occasion and like that they're gone."

He cupped her cheeks. "My job is not that dangerous. I'm sure it was horrible when you lost your brother, and I'm not minimizing that."

"I lost him and all I had was Edison, and he was off on another tour. I had to wait to really mourn my brother because there was no one else. When Edison returned he was already different. He was changing. He was abrupt, quiet, snappy over little things, and it got worse after each tour and being that perfect girlfriend who was supportive and accepting to it all I stayed," she said to him, and then pointed at her chest. "I stayed and I did everything in my power. I took hits. I took verbal and physical abuse. I took it all. I held him in my arms when he lost it at night, or just burst into tears thinking of how his entire troop was killed and he survived. I took him to places hoping to help him, and I went without eating three meals a day and making ends meet just to try and save him." She wrapped the towel around her body. He reached out to touch her and she pulled away.

"Kai, he hit you?" Thermo asked, standing in the doorway fully dressed and his hair wet from taking a shower she presumed. Selasi was there, too.

She took a deep breath and exhaled.

"I got a whole lot of fear. The three of you are exactly what I've been running from, what I fought so hard to resist, and it happened anyway."

"What we have is special, Kai. You can't ignore our connection to you and you to us. You can't deny how it felt to make love together," Selasi said to her.

She shook her head. "I'm not denying it. I just need the truth, for the three of you to be honest with me, and for you to be patient with me."

Thermo stuck out his hand. "Why don't you get dressed and we'll go out to grab a bite."

"Really?" she asked him.

"Even though we would rather stay here and have you for breakfast, lunch, and dinner," he said, and pulled her into his arms. She hugged him tight.

"Maybe stop at the hospital to see Devin?" she asked.

"Then breakfast first, stop to see Devin, bring back lunch to have here, and then have you," Selasi said, and she gave him a sassy look as she walked from the bathroom to the bedroom, and it earned her a slap to her ass, and a yank on her towel.

She tried covering herself up but Selasi wrapped his arm around her waist and threw her onto the bed, landing partially over her.

"Change of plans again. Have Kai again, then eat, then hospital, and then Kai all night long." He started tickling her until those tickles turned into kisses and then suckles, and soon she was placed on their liking before they made love to her again one more time. Selasi licked down her belly to her pussy.

She grabbed his head. "We're never getting out of here today, are we?" she asked and then moaned.

"We'll break for food. You'll need your energy, sweetie," Zayn said, pulling off his shirt and joining in.

She closed her eyes and absorbed the way it felt to be kissed by them, touched by them, shared by them and made love to by them, and the more she relaxed, the more she started to hope that this was real, and nothing bad would get in the way or ruin it. Nothing.

Chapter Ten

"Okay, start talking. How?" Afina asked Kai, grabbing onto her arm and walking down the hall of the hospital. Devin was finally starting to wake up for longer periods of time.

"It was crazy. They just showed up at my townhouse and basically Thermo demanded that I be honest. The next thing I know he's kissing me, and well…it was incredible." Kai glanced over her shoulder to see Thermo watching where she was going. It seemed he didn't like her out of his sights at all. She was happy for the first time in a very long time.

"That sounds so hot. They were probably pissed off because Mike said you were at that luncheon with Chadwick."

"Yeah, I figured as much, but even if they didn't come over, it wasn't like I was considering dating Chadwick."

"Really?" Afina raised her eyebrows up at Kai.

"Yes, really. Why don't you believe me?" she asked, and they took a seat in two chairs by the end of the door where Devin's room was. The doctor was in with him now and then they could all go in and visit him.

"Honey, I know you. Know what you've been through and how tough things have been over the years. You changed, closed up the second you got here to the hospital the night Devin was shot and Zayn, too. You went into your professional mode, talking to Chadwick, which thank God the man wants you in his bed or who knows what could have happened to Devin. Dr. McAndrews wasn't confident about surgery and needed a whole team to come in to assist.

I got the feeling you were pushing them away and thinking Chadwick would be the safer choice for you."

Kai clasped her hands on her lap after she crossed her legs. She glanced up at Afina. "That obvious?"

"Ahuh. So what happened?"

"The luncheon went awesomely. I mean completely amazing. I met some really wealthy, caring individuals who were impressed with what Guardians Hope is all about. They handed me checks for like ten thousand dollars, twenty thousand dollars, and I got volunteers and more interest in funding specific programs. Monday is going to be crazy for me."

"That is incredible. Oh my God, you'll be able to do so much."

"Planning it all out is key, having a board and working out the details together will be time-consuming but well worth it. We'll be able to reach so many clients. That idea about building the single small homes, those little cottages in a neighborhood for homeless vets can become a reality here in Mercy."

"It's an awesome idea. They seem to be successful in other parts of the country."

"I think they should be all over. Our veterans need our support."

Afina smiled at her. "The vets are lucky to have you as an advocate for them."

"You know this is what I love to do."

"So what happened with Chadwick?" she asked her.

"He leaves for Africa in a few days, but we came to an agreement."

"An agreement?"

"To remain friends."

"You told him about the guys?"

"He figured it out, but was trying to persuade me to meet him in Africa."

"What? Persuade you how?"

"When we got to my car after the luncheon, he grabbed me, pressed me up against the car and kissed me."

"He kissed you?" She raised her voice and Kai looked behind her and saw that Selasi, Zayn, and Thermo heard Afina. Mike, Turner and the others started walking their way.

"Shhh. Not a word. I pushed him away and well, we worked it out. Friends."

"Hot damn, woman. Well, I'm glad you're letting your guard down. So, a ménage huh? You naughty little thing. They're huge."

Afina blushed and then Kai felt the hand on her shoulder.

Selasi squinted at Kai. "Everything okay?"

"Perfect," she said and stood up just as the doctor came out and greeted them, and then let them go in to see Devin.

The moment she walked into the room she felt the tears fill her eyes. All the wires, the tubes, the beeping sounds got to her. He was resting, bandages along his arm chest and shoulder, but he was slightly sitting up. Afina went over first and kissed his forehead. His eyes blinked open.

"Hey, cus," she whispered. He gave a soft smile. "Everyone is here. Mike, Kai, Turner, Fogerty, Zayn, Thermo, and Selasi," she told him, and he looked past her.

"Kai," he whispered, and Afina stepped back.

Selasi gave Kai's hips a squeeze and she gripped his hand bringing Selasi forward with her. He kept a hand on her hip and remained close as she needed.

"Hey, handsome?" she said to Devin.

"I'm okay, Kai. I don't want you to be scared." Tears spilled from her eyes, her nose clogged up. He was shot and he was worried about her being scared.

She reached out and cupped his cheek. "Well, you did scare me."

"I knew I would be fine. You're an angel, Kai, and family." She lowered down and kissed his cheek.

"Selasi."

"You're doing good, cus. Keep fighting and every day you'll get stronger," Selasi said, and gave his good shoulder a squeeze. "The others want to say hello."

Kai smiled at him and stepped back, then listened to him talk softly to Zayn, asking him about his arm, as Selasi held her around her waist and kissed her shoulder. She squeezed his forearms and kept them tight around her waist, loving how it felt having him here protecting her. She listened to Devin tell Zayn he was glad his wound wasn't bad, and to take care of Kai, and said something else to Thermo that must have got to him because Thermo looked serious.

They only stayed for a little while because of the rules of short visits while he was recovering. They said good-bye to everyone and talked about meeting at Corporal's later tonight. Selasi said sure but Thermo said maybe. She looked at Zayn and even though he wore a long sleeve shirt she knew the bandage was underneath there. She held that hand, and leaned against his shoulder, kissing where the bandage was. He stopped her by the end of the hallway and turned, cupped her cheek and stared down into her eyes. "I'm okay."

She nodded. "I know."

He smiled then pressed his lips softly to hers. When he released her lips, they headed out of the hospital and to their truck. She slid along the seat next to Thermo. As Selasi drove and Zayn remained in the passenger seat, they recommended heading to their place so they could show her their home, the land they owned, and their own gym and dojo.

She glanced at Thermo. He was quiet, serious like usual, and she just stared at him, at his side profile, seeing how big he was. How large those tattooed, muscular arms were in the sleeveless flannel he wore. It was dark green and navy blue, it kind of brought out his eyes she noticed earlier, and would do so even more if he wasn't always frowning and squinting in anger. The jeans on his thighs were stretched to capacity. He had super big thighs and when they made love, she felt he could crush her if he put all his weight on her, but he didn't. He raised up and it wasn't until he came inside of her that he lowered, kissed her, and she felt how heavy and huge he was for a moment before he rolled her to her side. She felt aroused, needy and intimidated by him.

Despite making love so many times last night and this morning, she still felt a bit intimidated by each of the men, and significantly Thermo. Maybe because he had those scars he was hiding from her? Had PTSD and didn't want her to know? She did know, all too well the aftereffects of war on a man, on a soldier, but something inside of her told her it would be okay. She hesitated to touch him. To comfort him because of the fears of her past, of giving so much to Edison and it not being enough to save him. But Thermo didn't need saving. So why was she scared?

She reached over and put her hand on his thigh. It was hard as stone, and she felt him tighten, like her touch affected him, or perhaps he didn't want to be touched? Edison did that a lot, and it got worse and worse. Sometimes he would hold her close, but other times he would push her away. The tears emerged and she tried to hold them back. She started to pull her hand away, but he turned and grabbed her and lifted her onto his lap. "Thermo." She gasped, and held onto his shoulders and straddled his waist in the short beige flair skirt she wore. He pushed it to her hips and she lifted up, stared down into his dark, killer eyes, while he used his hands to massage her ass.

"I need you. All the time, every minute. I breathe in your scent, your shampoo, and feel you next to me and I need you again and again and again," he said to her.

She cupped his cheeks. "I feel that way, too." She lowered her mouth to his and kissed him, then felt his thick, hard digit press up into her cunt. She rocked her hips, riding that digit.

"We're almost there. When we get there it's right to the bedroom," Zayn said from the passenger seat.

She continued to kiss Thermo as he fingered her. She pecked at his lips, then his eyelids while he used his other hand to cup her breast and pinch her nipple. "Oh, Thermo, I want so badly that I ache."

"I ache, too, sweetie," he said as she panted against his lips and lifted higher while he pushed her top up and shoved her bra into an awkward position before latching onto her breast.

"Oh!" She gasped as the truck came to an abrupt stop. The engine died, doors opened.

"Now that is one sexy fucking sight," Selasi said as she looked at him, feeling her heavy eyelids, but she must have looked sexy because Selasi licked his lips and then Zayn slid into the backseat and pressed his hand over her ass cheek. He stroked down the crack.

"Let's get her inside, strip her down and fill her up," he said, then nipped her ass.

"Pass her over," Selasi said to Thermo.

"I got her." He grunted and she shivered from his tone and possessive words. He pulled his fingers from her cunt and she felt the loss. She actually moaned slightly and then he was sliding out of the truck, carrying her effortlessly as she tried pushing down her skirt but couldn't.

"No one can see. We own a lot of land, and the main road is nearly half a mile from our house," Zayn said to her.

She looked around them. Stunned at the beauty of the land, all open, with a large barn, and then a four car garage set up all decorated with landscaping around it, and the house. "Oh my God that is stunning," she whispered.

Their home was huge, with a large front porch, dark wood rocking chairs, half stone on the front instead of siding or wood, a gorgeous stained glass door with wrought iron bars that looked ancient. When they entered she barely registered the décor and setup. A fireplace, large sunken living room, and that was it, Thermo was practically running her up the staircase and then down the hallway. There were pictures on the walls, military, maybe family. It was a blur as he got her into a large bedroom, and she inhaled. It smelled like Thermo.

"Your room?" she asked, as he placed her feet on the bedroom floor, wide planked and dark wood, very rich looking yet masculine, as well.

He gripped her hips, pressed her skirt and panties down.

"Yes," he said in a deep tone that made her nipples hard.

"Arms up," he ordered, and she raised them up slowly as he gripped her top, and pulled it up over her head. She sensed someone on the bed behind her, then felt the fingers unclipping her bra. She nearly moaned, as the cups of her bra lowered, releasing her very sensitive breasts. They lifted the bra off of her and there she stood, arms in the air, fully naked.

Thermo licked his lips. His hands on her hips, so warm and large, seared her skin.

"You're everything to me," he said to her. She held his gaze.

Zayn kissed her shoulder from behind and lowered her arms then pulled them behind her. Her voice hitched as he restrained her, and she felt his thick, hard cock against her spine. "Everything to the three of us."

Thermo undid his pants and stepped from them. He lowered down and kissed her breasts. She closed her eyes and tilted toward his mouth.

"So sexy and all ours, always," Selasi said, and he cupped her cheek. She blinked her eyes open just as his lips covered hers. She closed her eyes again and absorbed their tactics, the way they played her body so well, and made her feel so deeply.

Thermo continued to explore her with his mouth, sucking her nipple on one side then the other before going lower and suckling against her hip bone and then the tattoo he seemed to like so much. He had a lot of tattoos. Would he want her to get another one? Maybe their names, marking her, branding her so she belonged to only them forever? Her pussy clenched and she moaned into Selasi's mouth, just as Thermo's mouth and beard made contact with her cunt. She swayed.

"Legs apart," Zayn said, suckling on her neck as his fingers slid into her cunt then over her anus. They worked her body together. Selasi released her lips and lowered to feast on her breast. She rocked her hips.

"Please," she begged.

"Tell us what you want?" Thermo said, and slid his wet digit into her asshole, just as Thermo thrust his tongue into her cunt.

"All of you inside of me. Please, Zayn, Thermo, Selasi. Please."

Thermo pulled his mouth from her cunt. Selasi released her breast and Zayn released her wrists and slid his finger from her ass. She gasped and teetered where she was.

"I'll grab the lube," Zayn said, and stepped away.

"Together," Selasi said, and stroked her cheek, cupping it. She leaned into it and closed her eyes.

"Kai," Thermo said her name and she opened her eyes to look at him as Selasi released her cheek, and Zayn now stood on Thermo's other side.

"No more secrets or fears," Thermo said to her, then he reached for the buttons on his shirt. She inhaled, shocked at what she believed he was going to reveal, to trust her with. His brothers seemed surprised, too, and now their expressions were hard, serious, and she gulped. The shirt was undone and as he shifted out of it she saw the deep, pink gashes all over his chest, his stomach. There were so many. Too many and they seemed to trail along the sides and to his back.

She got emotional and he went to turn away and she grabbed his hips and pressed her lips to his chest. She started to kiss each line, and heard his intake of breath, felt his one hand on her shoulder slide under her neck and hair and grip, while his other grabbed her hip and he tilted back as if her kisses affected every part of him. She loved him. She loved the three of them and she knew it, right now, in this moment, that this was so special and real.

She didn't want him focusing on the scars or her reaction, she wanted him focusing on her lips, the feel of her mouth on him and she swirled her tongue over his nipple and nipped and tugged hard.

"Fuck." He grunted.

She went lower and lower, and his thick, hard fingers gripped her hair tight and she took his cock into her mouth and began to suck on him. She looked up and he watched her cock slide in and out of her mouth and so did his brothers. They appeared hungry, carnal, and Zayn was tapping the tube of lube on his palm, and her asshole clenched in anticipation of being filled with cock. She moaned and she came. Just like that she came.

"Get up here now," Thermo demanded and pulled out of her mouth.

Thermo lifted her up into his arms and kissed her then lowered her to the bed. He ravished her mouth and then pressed her arms up above her and she obeyed. He trailed his mouth down her body over her breasts then to her cunt. He lifted her thighs up over his shoulders bringing her to her shoulder blades and he licked her from cunt to asshole, back and forth lubricating both entrances and she moaned another release. He reached his hand out and Zayn squeezed lube onto his finger and Thermo pressed it to her anus. "Oh." She moaned but she didn't take her eyes off of Thermo or that dominate, in control expression he had right now.

"Mine," he said to her, and then he pulled his finger from her anus and replaced it with his cock. He slid right in and she moaned, was gasping at the feel of him filling her up in this position. Her shoulders the only part of her on the end of the bed, her legs over his forearms and he thrust into her asshole.

She cried out, rolled her head side to side and then Zayn was over her belly, licking his way to her breast and then sliding his finger into her cunt.

It was so erotic and wild.

"We need in," Selasi said.

Thermo thrust two more times and then slowly pulled out of her ass, lowered her to the bed and she felt the loss, but then he lifted her up as if she weighed nothing at all. He kissed her then turned her around abruptly, placing her over Zayn, and she slid her pussy over his cock and immediately began to ride him. Thermo lowered her down and once again his cock slid into her asshole slowly, letting her adjust to the two cocks, but she was more than adjusted to being penetrated in every hole. She yearned for it, begged to be filled by the three of them. Selasi was on the bed and she lifted up and opened her mouth.

"God damn I love you," he said to her and then lifted his cock to her mouth and she took him in. They all worked their cocks into her together, and she didn't try to focus on moving in three directions. She focused on the sensations, the feelings of being complete, protected and loved. "I love you, baby," Selasi said, and then grunted and came.

"I love this ass, and I love you," Thermo said to her and he came next.

He slid out and then Selasi pulled his cock from her mouth, and Zayn passed her to him and he lowered her to the bed, spread her thighs and Selasi slid his cock right into her cunt and began to thrust into her. He held her shoulders, getting better leverage, and she cried out at how deeply he was inside of her and she came.

"So fucking good. So good. I love you," he said, and then came inside of her. Selasi lowered to the crook of her neck and suckled and kissed her. He released her arms and she hugged him, felt him crush her to the bed, and she grunted before he rolled to the side.

"I could crush you," he said, sliding his palm up and down her belly, her ribs and then to her breast, cupping it.

"I love how it feels when each of you hold me in your arms, how you let go after coming inside of me and I feel all your weight for a few seconds. It makes me feel sexy and protected," she admitted.

"You are sexy, and you are protected," Zayn said, and brought her fingers to his lips and kissed her knuckles.

Thermo lay on the bed next to her, no longer wearing a shirt, and he gave a soft smile. It shocked her. "I…" She swallowed hard and they all had a hand on her and she lay there looking up at the three of them.

"I love each of you, too. I never thought I would ever love again. I was too scared to love again, but then the three of you came along and…I don't feel alone anymore." she said, and her eyes welled up with tears.

Thermo caressed her hair and then leaned over and kissed her shoulder. "I don't feel alone anymore either," he said, and they all remained together, making love into the evening until the texts messages about joining the others became too annoying to ignore.

Chapter Eleven

"So it's official then? You three and Kai?" Mike asked Selasi, Thermo, and Zayn as they bought another round of beers.

"It's official," Selasi said, and then looked toward the right where Kai was talking to Amelia, North, Melina, and April. Mike watched as one of the cops he knew that was friends with Devin walked by and said hello to North. He placed his hand on her hip and whispered something to her and North rolled her eyes and then stepped to the side. She wasn't dating anyone. At least not that he knew of. He took another sip from his beer.

"How about you? Thinking of making a move yet?" Zayn asked him and smirked.

He squinted. "Making a move on who?" he asked.

"A tall, sexy blonde in real estate," Selasi added. Was it that obvious that Mike had his eyes on North? Of course he couldn't make a move. Phantom was resistant, Turner already focusing on the next mission that would bring them away for two weeks minimum, and they knew it wouldn't be fair to start something. Phantom wasn't the commitment type at all.

"Did Turner talk to you, Selasi, about some stuff we need that's coming up?" he asked, changing the subject.

Selasi chuckled and then looked toward the women. "I know you're changing the subject and all, but I wouldn't wait too long, or you could miss another opportunity to see where things lead," Selasi said.

"Hey listen, just because you three fell head over heels for Kai, doesn't mean you start taking on a matchmaking role here. You'll lose friends like that, man. Guys like us don't do commitments. We never know when we have to leave for the next job, and you know as well as I do the danger we're in," Mike said, and then he glanced again at the women and then saw Casey and Kai walking toward the ladies room. He looked at Thermo, Zayn, and Selasi and they watched, too.

"Sure you don't want to follow her and hold her hand?" he teased.

They turned away and toward the bar. "You can fuck with us all you want right now, but one day you'll see how this shit just fucking takes over. That there's this protective, possessive sensation that only goes down to a simmer when she's right there in your arms. It's insane," Zayn said, and Mike chuckled, then they heard a gunshot.

* * * *

Casey showed Kai her phone and the text messages from Lionel.

They were by the back hallway and the doorway.

"We need to call the police. Hell, the place is swarming with cops. This is serious, Casey," Kai said to her.

"I don't understand it. Why is he allowed to be out of jail after what he did to me and the charges I pressed? This isn't even like the man I knew, that I dated for nearly a year. I think it's the drugs."

"Drugs?"

"I think he started using."

"Damn it, Casey. He could be high or something. That assault charge was a slap on the wrist and considered minor, but this is stalking and harassment, a threat to your life," Kai said.

"I'm so scared, Kai," Casey replied as tears fell.

Kai hugged her. "Don't let anyone see. Please, can we talk to someone we can trust? Someone who won't make a scene here?" she asked, and they walked toward the back door.

"Of course we can. Zayn can help," Kai told her.

It was instant. The sound of a gunshot, the glass shattered hitting both of them, but Casey was on the ground, bleeding, and Kai was stunned. She looked up and Lionel was there. Bloodshot eyes, gun on her and then Casey then back on her.

"Freeze right there!"

She turned to look and there were multiple men with their guns drawn. Ghost, Mike, Zayn, and Phantom. She couldn't move. She feared Lionel would kill her.

She looked down at Casey who was moaning with her hand against her shoulder. Kai was bleeding on her arms, the glass that shattered hit her there and on her neck, against her chest. She was shaking, but then Lionel grabbed her and pulled her against his chest, the gun under her chin.

"Don't!" Zayn yelled to him.

"Please, Lionel. Don't do this. We can talk about this."

"We aren't talking." His words were slurred and he was shaking as he held her. She stared straight ahead at her men, at her friends and they looked so intense. Zayn was moving like he wanted to shoot. Could she move fast enough for him to take a shot? The hallway was so small.

"Get up, Casey!" he yelled at her, right next to Kai's ear. She tightened her eyes. He kicked Casey.

"Don't do that to her," Kai pleaded, and then looked at Zayn, at Thermo, and Selasi. She stared at them hoping they could tell her what to do.

"Don't move," Zayn lipped to her.

Lionel was looking back through the doorway.

"Tell them to get away or I'll shoot both of them. I don't fucking care. I'll kill them!" Lionel yelled.

"Tell whomever is out there to get back!" Ghost yelled to the crowd behind them, and then Mike was telling everyone to move out. Sirens blared in the distance and she knew this situation was getting worse by the second. Casey tried getting up as Lionel kicked her again and again.

Kai grabbed onto his thighs. "Don't, Lionel. Please don't do this. She couldn't see his face, but he pulled her to the wall so his back was against it. He stared straight ahead and the last thing she expected was for him to put his mouth on her shoulder. She gasped.

"She's one of yours, right. How does it feel to know I can take her away from you pigs?" he asked, thinking that she was with one of the cops. He licked her neck and she cringed and shook with anger now. She was breathing through her nostrils.

She went to move and he pressed the barrel of the gun to her throat. Tears filled her eyes and a fear so great had her heart pounding in her chest.

"Let her go, Lionel. Put the gun down, give up and the only charge will be you replacing my window," Ghost said to him.

Lionel chuckled and snorted. It was obvious he was high. She felt the strap to her bra and camisole begin to fall from the way he was holding her. His other arm was tight around her waist, then his hand was sliding up to her breast.

"Lionel, let her go and I'll go with you," Casey said, still laying on the floor, looking pale and weak. He didn't even seem to care about her anymore.

"I think I found a new toy."

"Don't you fucking touch her!" Selasi yelled at him, and Lionel laughed and cupped her breast.

She was breathing through her nostrils, saw the men breathing heavy, heard their mumbled curses as Lionel fondled her breast and she was pissed when she caught Thermo's eyes.

"No, Kai," Zayn said to her, but she wasn't going to stand here and let the man fondle her breast. When he placed his mouth against her neck, she leaned her head back as she used her hands to rub his thighs, tilted her hips forward, making him lose focus, and slid her palm over his crotch.

"What the fuck?" He exhaled and moved the gun and she made her move.

Twisting out of his hold, she slammed the gun from his hand, forearmed him to the throat and then knocked him in the nose, breaking his nose. The gun went flying and then she slammed her knee into his stomach, and he fell onto his back and then strong arms pulled her back as the other men flipped him over and cuffed him.

She struggled a moment as Zayn hugged her as well as Thermo and Selasi. They were caressing her hair and she was hugging them back.

"Holy fuck, woman. What the hell were you thinking?" Zayn yelled at her, but squeezed her tighter. She tilted up with tears in her eyes and he kissed her lips. "Get her away from here. Away from that piece of shit," Thermo said in anger.

"Wait, Casey," she said.

"They got her. The paramedics are here," Selasi said.

Ghost looked at Kai. "You waited kind of long, Kai. A few more seconds, and Jesus," he said and shook his head.

"The gun was to my throat," she replied.

"No one would believe how you got out of that. Glad I have cameras," he said and pointed up.

"Wonderful, now everyone can see how she grabbed Lionel by the balls, fondling him so she could make a move," Mike said.

She looked at Thermo. He reached for her hand and then cursed. She cringed as she stretched it.

"Looks like Casey isn't the only one going to the hospital," Selasi said to her.

She hugged Thermo, kept her face against his chest and just breathed in his scent, his cologne and the feeling of protection him and his brothers instantly provided. The chaos continued around them. The police on the scene, Lionel still flipping out, but battered and beaten by her, a broken nose and he was going to jail. Thermo tried walking her away, but Lionel was no longer in the hallway and she wanted to check on Casey.

"Casey."

"You did more than enough. You saved her life and nearly got fucking killed. I don't want you away from me," Thermo said. She held his hand and pulled him with her. He exhaled. The paramedics had Casey on a gurney right there by the back entrance.

"Kai. Oh God, I'm so sorry this happened."

She caressed her cheek. "It wasn't your fault, but it's over now."

"Thank God you're trained the way you are, Kai."

"A soldier's woman, a cop's sister, never forgets her training. We'll follow you to the hospital," she said, and Casey nodded and then Kai turned into Thermo's arms and hugged him again. Selasi looked at her hand and she gazed up at him.

"Can you wiggle your fingers?" he asked.

"It's fine," she said but as she tried, she cringed.

"Let me see," Turner said, and came over. He apparently was some sort of medic on his team as a mercenary.

"I think you may have broken something," he said to her.

"Should have killed the fucker," Selasi stated.

"Emergency room. Let's go," Zayn said.

"Could I maybe take a shower first?" she asked.

"What? Why the hell would you want to shower first?" Mike asked her.

"I can feel Lionel on my neck. He licked me and suckled there and—"

"Enough! We saw it. Let's get to the hospital, get the x-ray and when we're done we take you home, you shower and then we spend the rest of the fucking weekend in bed," Thermo stated in front of everyone. Then he lifted her up into his arms and carried her away. The guys all cheered, hooted and hollered and she didn't mind at all as Selasi and Zayn followed, shaking their heads and still looking angry. They all would need a lot of hugs and kisses tonight, and she would need all three of her men deep inside of her, making love to her, keeping her close, and making her feel whole again.

"I love you guys," she said to them, and kissed Thermo's neck.

"We love you, too, but when we get home later, you're getting your first ass spanking for getting caught in that situation and for scaring the life out of us," Zayn said.

"What?" she asked.

"I second that," Selasi said, opening the truck door.

"Ooh Rah!" Thermo added, and his brothers chuckled and she felt her body's reaction to their words, and their show of possession, protection and desire. Who would have thought that the type of men she had been running from and fearing would be the ones she fell in love with? This warrior angel found her very own warriors to call her own.

THE END

WWW.DIXIELYNNDWYER.COM

Siren Publishing, Inc.
www.SirenPublishing.com

Lightning Source UK Ltd.
Milton Keynes UK
UKHW01f1046160718
325772UK00006B/1010/P